THE DEAD WOODS

CHRISTIAN FRANCIS

Special thank you to
Ken Winkler and Janine Pipe

E-book: 978-1-916582-00-2
Paperback: 978-1-916582-02-6
Hardcover: 978-1-916582-04-0

ECHO ON
PUBLISHING

echohorror.com

ADVANCE PRAISE
FOR 'THE DEAD WOODS'

I will never recover from this book. Thank you!

— JAMIE C - NETGALLEY

I loved this book! It gave me Stranger Things meets My Best Friends Exorcism meets IT vibes, but the author took the best parts of these and created something totally new!

— KRISTENSTRATTON0810 - BOOK
SIRENS

...some parts made me sad whereas others kept me glued and turning the pages with lightning speed. And that ending...score.

— SUGARC - GOODREADS

Such an awesome twist on the haunted woods/creature in the woods trope. Combining horror and science fiction, Christian Francis hit it out of the ballpark with *The Dead Woods*, it was gripping, atmospheric, and unique.

— REGINA S - NETGALLEY

Well-crafted horror story. Just what I needed. I was in search of a horror story and luckily found this gem.

— MAVIS S LIBRARIAN - NETGALLEY

A fantastic entry to the horror scene... The ending certainly was a twist! All in all, this was a book I couldn't put down once I started it.

— KATE - BOOK SIRENS

This book was like a creepy campfire story past down from generation after generation. Anyone sitting around a fire deep in the woods wouldn't sleep after hearing this one! Beware the tree man.

— CHRISTEN E - NETGALLEY

A combination of Stephen King's IT, Fear Street, and a little bit of Stranger Things... I love the vibe!

— REVIEWER 1140317 - NETGALLEY

For Vicky
xxx

CONTENTS

PROLOGUE

1985

They say I should never unlock my window. They tell me I should keep the curtains closed at night. It's been so hard, but I miss Bixley *so much*.

They told me he died. They told me they saw the body. They told me they buried him.

They are *liars*!

I saw him, and I keep telling them they are wrong.

He has been visiting me at night. Sitting outside my window whimpering. I want to let him in so badly. But they won't give me the key to open it.

My parents tell me I'm making up stories. They say the same things over and over. *He hasn't come back. He's gone. Now go to bed and stop lying.* But when I ask them why they don't come and see for themselves, they just change the subject. *You wouldn't understand. When you're older. It's too adult. Do what you're told.*

Well, *to hell* with what they say.

Tonight though, I hope he returns, wagging his tail as always. And if he does, I plan to let him. You see, I stole the key to the window. I'll wait until the moon is at its fullest when all the sunlight has been chased away. When the yellow mist from the woods covers our lawn and seeps in through the window vent, I'll see Bixley. Tiny, perfect Bixley, his smooth black fur looking wet and matted, begging to be dried and cut. He must be so sad.

He looked in at me, showing his shiny teeth like he was smiling at me, happy to see me, begging to come in.

They'll believe me when I show them my baby boy is alive and has come home.

They can't make me leave him outside again for another night.

He's been gone for so long.

Sure, he's not quite like before. But he *is* Bixley. I can't wait to see him smiling his little puppy smile again.

Tonight, I'm opening the window wide and letting him come home. I don't care what anyone says. I don't want to have another night without him. And when I *do* bring him inside, after I dry him off, Bixley and I shall lie on my bed together, warm and snug, like we always used to do.

I will rub him behind his ears until he falls asleep and dreams his little puppy dreams. My baby Bixley. He always—

I hear him.

I hear him.

I hear his little scratches on the glass.

As I open the curtains, there he is again... smiling, waiting.

I unlock the window.

I turn the handle.

I—

OH NO.... please God, NO!

HIS LAST ROUTE

1989

"Adam Petrie, *that* was his name!" James exclaimed as his face lit up. He shot to his feet with a victorious smile and turned to his friends, all sitting in a circle on the clubhouse floor, staring back at him. "Right?" he asked. "Adam Petrie?" He clicked his fingers victoriously, just as he always did when he made any exclamations—a minor peccadillo he had picked up from his father.

Though thirteen, James passed for much younger. And when he smiled his biggest, happiest smile—as he did now —he looked no older than ten or eleven.

"Adam?" Findley was the first to respond as he nodded. "Yeah. That was it. Adam Petrie." His expression turned quizzical. "Weird we *totally* forgot his name, right?" His voice trailed off as he spoke more to himself than his friends. "It wasn't *that* long ago."

James Tran and Findley Scott had been best friends for as far back as they could remember. James and his family moved to Hemlock Creek when he was only six. He didn't remember much about his years in Los Angeles, except for his first days at Our Lord of Light Elementary, where a big bully with a pimpled face picked on him relentlessly for his Vietnamese features, saying he wasn't a real American.

"You look yellow. You *are* yellow. You should get out of my country!" Evan Walsh told him. "My dad said–"

Findley watched this scene play out in disgust, as James shrank in the bully's shadow, his body trembling.

3

Findley watched this happening and saw James looking more scared by the second. He could not let it play out as it usually would with Evan. Findley *had* to jump in.

Pushing himself between Evan and James. He met the bully's stare straight-on and cut him off mid-sentence. "Hey, Evan, you *look* like a butt. You *are* a butt. So, go puke a turd and get out of his face!" he said with as much threat as he could verbally muster.

Not knowing what else to do, the bully relented. Findley was as tall as he was, and though dumb as a post regarding school, the bully had a modicum ofsense when it came to his own preservation. At least he did for that day. Of course, the bullying continued, but at least he'd won James a respite.

James had asked, on many occasions, why Findley protected him from Evan. But his friend just shrugged and always answered in the same way. "I hated him." James liked to think it was because Findley was a kind-hearted person, but his friend would never accept such a compliment.

From then on, Findley and James stuck together. Over the years, from Elementary to Middle School, they had formed a small group of friends. Small but perfect all the same, at least that's what James thought.

First was Emmie Hanson. A year younger, with more attitude than all her friends combined. She hated the label her parents gave her, *tomboy*, as she was not a boy. She hated the thought of being one. But she also hated the idea of being a girl. She liked to call herself a *middler*: happy being both but neither. Out of the whole group, she was the bravest by far. She was the first to cross the bridge at Edson Dam. The first to explore the mineshaft they found last summer on the ridge behind the Weybrook Farm. She would even run into a burning house if someone dared her.

The second was Hamish Flynn. A boy who liked to think he was the group's clown but was really just the most normal one of them. He always tried to make everyone laugh but lacked Findley's sense of humor, James' intelligence, and Emmie's boldness. He was... Hamish. Dependable. Nice. Caring. Friendly. Hamish. He looked up to everyone in the group, sensing they were somehow sharper and more mature. He tried his best to hide his feelings of inadequacy, playing instead for likability, hence the bad jokes and goofy comments. And they did seem to like him, didn't they?

Third was Philip Kaminsky Jr., known as Pip, to avoid confusion with his father—the town Priest. With his mother being a funeral director, Pip was something of a black sheep in his own mind. He didn't believe in God, no matter what his father tried to instill in him, and he was petrified of death, no matter what his mother said to calm his fears. He often wondered if he was adopted, but Pip could not look more like his father if he tried. He felt like a mental rebel, hampered by being painfully shy. He could never tell his father his true beliefs, or lack of them. He would never let his mother know how much the darker side of her work upset him. All those bodies, lying still in their caskets, flowers everywhere. He hated the smell of flowers. He knew he lied to them, but believed he did so for the right reasons. He was filled with strong opinions but kept them all inside. He didn't want to hurt anyone. He had embraced this idealized version of himself and played it with aplomb.

James, Findley, Emmie, Hamish, and Pip. Inseparable.

. . .

"WHO THE HELL IS ADAM PETRIE?" Emmie asked, having zoned out of the last conversation completely.

"The kid," Findley said. "The one found dead in his bedroom. He was in our year. Pip's mom said it was an animal."

Pip swallowed hard. The conversation took a turn he'd rather avoid. But, as ever, he was too polite to say anything about it.

"You *gotta* remember him?" James said, with a grin as wide as it could go. He was so happy with remembering the poor boy's name, when no one else did, that he could not hide his visible satisfaction. "We were in fourth grade together?"

"I was in grade three, genius," Emmie mumbled with a sour expression.

"The kid whose dog went missing," Hamish cut in. "Mr. Prest made us put up those missing posters on lunch break."

Emmie's eyes widened as she suddenly remembered. "Oh... God... *Bixley*!"

"Huh?" James said, his smile slipping. Findley looked just as confused.

"That dog!" Emmie looked around. "I remember the poster... *Find my Bixley*? I saw that poster every day for months. That was *that* kid's dog?"

Emmie turned to Pip. "What did your mom say? What about an animal?" she asked, nudging his leg.

Pip, tight-lipped, shook his head. "She didn't say much," he paused before finding the courage to continue. "Just it may be... I dunno, it was a while ago."

James leaned back on the wooden wall of their clubhouse. "Your mom said it was some animal that got him. Bites all over his body!"

Pip shrugged and nodded. "She said they were cuts. They looked like bites. I dunno what she meant."

"We all thought his dog had come back to get revenge," James smiled. "So stupid."

"They found Bixley in Edson Dam a few weeks before, right?" Emmie asked. "Been dead a while."

"I don't like thinking about any of this." Pip shrugged.

"So, his dog went missing, kicked the bucket at the dam," Findley said. "Then Adam died, and people thought the dog came back from the grave and killed him?"

"Bixley," Emmie cut in.

"What kind of name is Bixley, anyway?" James laughed.

"Fine, *Bixley* came back and then did that to Adam?" Findley replied. "That's so lame."

"It wasn't a dog," Hamish said with certainty. "I read about it in the paper. Said it was natural causes. A heart thingy or something. The dog stuff was just gossip. Your mom wasn't right—"

"My mom wasn't lying!" Pip said as he shot Hamish a harsh glance. "She saw Adam's body. The reporter didn't!"

Quickly, as the penny dropped, Hamish turned to Adam, shocked. "I—I'm sorry. I didn't mean she lied. I was just—"

"Of course, the papers didn't say it was an animal. Murdered in his own bedroom by an animal?" James said. "Nah, they wouldn't want people panicking. I believe Pip's mom. That's an inside scoop right there."

Findley quickly checked his watch. "Ah, flitsticks," he exclaimed. "It's six already."

Flitsticks, one of the many words Findley would use in place of swearing to avoid trouble from school administrators and his parents. The words sounded dirty in his mind, but out of his mouth, they sounded ridiculous, often annoying his friends to no end. But heck, it kept him out of detention. A method he had used for so long that he no longer considered swearing and only used his made-up words out of habit. Something that quietly annoyed his friends.

Emmie rolled her eyes. "Six? How's that even possible? We *just* got here!"

But they hadn't. They'd been sitting in the shed in the back of Hamish's house for over four hours—a place they dubbed The Clubhouse. Hamish's parents seemed more than happy to move the gardening equipment to their basement, knowing Hamish and his friends were nearby and safe, rather than up to mischief in the rougher parts of town.

Each of their parents were happy with this arrangement and were more than willing to shell out a few bucks so their children could decorate the small wooden building into something homier.

Findley had bought the paint with his pocket money from the local store—a garishly bright red paint.

James had convinced his parents to let him take the guest bedroom's television.

Emmie had taken an old rug from the garage.

Hamish had found some chairs at the local flea market his parents dragged him around every Sunday.

Pip bought a mini fridge, one his father said was broken, but they could use it to store things away from prying mice.

Ultimately, this clubhouse was theirs, and that was all that mattered. It was a place they could hide out in and talk about anything and everything as they sat in a circle on the rug.

Sure, they had intended to get the TV fixed, to get the mini-fridge fixed. Even buy some games to play. But they were very content, as they only needed a space to hang out.

As they walked home, each of them remembered Adam Petrie. Even Emmie. Though she feigned not knowing his name, she remembered him all too well. She loved to be contrary for the sake of it. *Everyone* in the group had known Adam. Each had spoken to him on occasion. Though none of them had ever been close friends, each had felt a pang of sadness at his passing. Sure, they had not kept his memory alive, but as soon as they heard James utter his name, it all came flooding back. Including the rumors of Bixley, and what he may have done to Adam.

The winter sun was quickly setting as the five of them parted ways, making their respective paths home. Dark shadows crawled over Hemlock Creek as the light turned orange and faded to nothing.

Findley and James lived the furthest away, on the other side of town. As the rest of the group were warm in their homes, the remaining two trod the chilly streets toward Fragrant Pines. This was a poetic name for the estate of tract housing they lived in. A place more affectionately dubbed 'Stinky Trees' by nearly every person who did *not* live there. Fragrant Pines was a nice-sounding place for a less-than-desirable part of town.

Crossing the disused railroad line, James walked on autopilot as he stepped over its metal tracks, ensuring he wouldn't get electrocuted. Not that he would, as they had not been used for decades. Findley, however, stepped on both tracks as he crossed over them, almost mocking James' needless caution. And this was what they did nearly every day they walked home.

James was preoccupied in his thoughts as they passed the Fragrant Pines entrance sign. After a few moments, he glanced around to Findley, with a weary expression. "You think Adam Petrie was *really* killed by his dog? Is it even possible? A zombie dog?"

Findley shrugged. "Man, I got no idea. Maybe it's possible? That dog could've had rabies. Gone insane like in the movie... Or another animal could have done it." He noticed the growing look of fear on his friend's face and changed tack, "Or, and I hate to be the one to say this... so, just hear me out."

They both slowed, as Findley explained.

"Now I love Pip as much as anyone. You know that, right?" he prefaced. "But he isn't always... Well... *that* concerned with telling the truth, if you get my meaning?"

James didn't reply. He just listened wide-eyed, trying to figure everything out silently.

Findley continued. "Remember when he said his dad found that Ouija board in the church?"

James nodded with a thin smile as he realized what Findley was about to say.

"Remember me *asking* his dad about it when we went over for lunch?"

"I forgot about the Ouija board," James agreed with a sheepish chuckle. "But it *was* a good story, right? Even if it wasn't true."

"Sure, and we never said anything to Pip. But you *know* that's how he is," Findley looked for the right words. "He...

He exaggerates stuff sometimes. Don't think it's a bad thing. Petrie died, yeah. It was horrible. The papers said it was a heart thingamajig. I *think* we can take their word on it, don't you? Why would they cover it up? And besides, Pip's mom isn't a doctor. She just puts 'em in the ground, and we only have his word for it that she said all the stuff about his dog."

It sounded plausible enough to James. He shrugged, and said, "I guess you're right."

Living one street apart, their houses backed up onto each other. A row of trees and high fencing separated their yards, blocking the view between their windows. Walking down Peach Blossom Court, they high-fived and went their separate ways home.

"Watch out for those killer dogs," Findley called back as he turned the corner home.

Hearing this, James felt a shiver creep down his body. He didn't reply. He swallowed as he glanced around at the shadows between his neighbors' homes. He half-expected a vicious spaniel to come running out at him, bloodthirsty and murderous, wanting to take him the same way as Adam Petrie.

After he closed the front door behind him, James' breathing calmed. He knew it was all a lie, but that didn't stop him from being overly cautious, just in case.

A scrambling of paws suddenly echoed franticly on the floorboards.

A slobbering mouth opened wide as it exited the living room.

"Arthur, no!" James exclaimed, as the Trans' Great Dane jumped up at him. Its two front paws landed on James' shoulders with a heavy thud. "Get off me!" he said, trying to lift the excitable weight off him.

But Arthur wanted to lick its owner. Lick him a *lot*.

Fear gave way to laughter as Arthur, the extremely drooly dog who stood taller than James on his hind legs, proceeded to drool all over him, licking every inch of James' face. And James happily allowed this to happen.

"WHAT IS IT, PIP?" Sarah Kaminsky asked with concern as she noticed her son's dour expression.

A spoonful of meatballs slopped onto Pip's plate, and he felt his stomach turn. He stared at the lumps of cooked flesh before him as they soaked in their boiling tomatoey juice. His only thoughts as he looked down at the food were of his dead classmate and the unbelievable stories about his passing.

Reverend Philip Kaminsky looked over, wearing a matching expression of concern. "Son?" he asked.

Sarah placed the spoon back in the serving dish and put her hand on Pip's forehead.

"I hope you're not coming down with anything," she said as he turned to her husband. "There's a bug going around. The LaFlamés have all come down with it."

"I'm okay," Pip said weakly with a tinge of annoyance. "It's... We were talking—"

"Who *are* we?" his father asked with a raised eyebrow.

"My friends."

"Yeah?" Sarah returned to her seat, the concerned expression not leaving her face.

Pip couldn't break his stare at the meat on his plate. "We talked about Adam Petrie."

Philip closed his eyes and shook his head. Sarah smiled through her gritted teeth. "Oh really, Adam Petrie?"

She glanced at her husband, and they shared a knowing look.

"That was quite a while ago," his father said. He meant it to be comfortingly, but it sounded condescending.

"What was said, baby?" Sarah asked in a kind yet worried tone.

Pip shrugged. "Nothing much. Just brought it up. I'd forgotten all about him." Pip then looked confused. "How did I forget it? I knew him, and he *died*. You'd think I'd always remember."

"Eat up," Sarah said dismissively. "We shouldn't be dwelling on something so sad, and as your dad said, it *was* so long ago."

"It was a dog, wasn't it?" Pip asked his mother with a crack in his voice. "That's what you said. A dog attacked him. You saw bites. D'you know what type? Was it *his* dog? I heard you saying it *looked* like a dog, but his died—"

"I didn't say bites," Sarah replied. "I said *looked like* bite patterns. How do you even know what I said?"

"I heard you speaking to the Sheriff," Pip replied meekly.

"Whatever happened no longer matters," Philip interrupted. "Adam Petrie is with God now. All that does matter is his soul's at rest. And Adam's not alone up there. His dad passed in the mill fire a few years ago... So, Adam has *his* father as well as his *heavenly* father."

Pip felt a pang of guilt as he heard his father's words and silently dismissed them as gibberish. All he could reply was, "I know." But he did *not* know. He wasn't bothered with the afterlife, but with what was left behind. Adam's father died, but his mother did not, and his mother remained in the family house. Alone. Pip passed it every week on his paper route. Delivering the Hemlock Gazette to her door. He now realized why she always looked so sad when he saw her—so haunted. That's what bothered Pip. Not only her boy dying. Not the gossip suggesting Adam's dead dog killed him. Not even the father dying so soon after. But mainly, it was the mother being left alone that bothered him. Alone in her house full of ghosts.

Pip looked at the meatballs and imagined Adam's mother right now. In her kitchen on her own, eating a dinner-for-one at a large empty table. His heart broke thinking of her loss.

But Pip would never say any of this aloud.

"Eat up," his mom said. "You must be starving."

The Reverend changed the subject, "Did I tell you both I saw Abner Grady's new kittens today?"

Pip ignored his thoughts and smiled at his father—a believable, yet phony smile.

As the sun crested over the horizon, Emmie was already awake.

Her bedside clock radio read 7:04 am, playing classical music over its small speakers.

Staring out of her bedroom window, Emmie smiled as she watched the world awaken. She stared as the light bounced over Cromwell Woods on the east side of town and crawled its way across the houses, toward her.

This was her morning ritual. The way to chase her demons away. The demons who invaded her mind at night, scaring her awake multiple times before dawn. These same demons who told her that she was a freak. The demons who said she was not good enough. The demons that made her feel useless.

Recently, it was at this time of the morning that she would feel sadness for the year to come; the year her friends would go to High School and she would stay in Middle School. She felt a deep fear about everything changing, leaving her behind, alone—Just like it was in her home.

"Emmaleen?" came the familiar voice of her father from downstairs.

She did not reply, as she knew what would follow. It was the same every morning. Words she mouthed along as her father shouted up the stairs to her.

"See you later. Love you."

This oft-repeated phrase was a specter of what it once was. It used to comfort her, but now it rang so hollow.

Only two years ago, things were different. Her bedroom door used to open. Her father used to walk in and kiss her on the forehead, hug her, and say those very words. But now, *now* it had all changed for the worse. *He* had changed. Since her mother died, taken by that horrible illness, her father had become a virtual ghost. Sure, he still looked like her father and talked like her father. But he was a broken, grief-consumed man. He tried to be there for her, and she knew he tried. He did love her, and she knew that too. But she also knew her mother's death was too much for him to deal with.

Emmie had tried on many occasions to talk to him. To try and get through to him. But her father was shut off emotionally. The words he called up the stairs were merely a reflex of a memory.

As she pushed back the tears threatening to break

through, she smiled as she saw Pip on his paper route a few streets away—riding his bike, snaking his way through the streets, throwing his papers at houses as he went.

WITH CROMWELL WOODS looming up behind the row of houses ahead, Pip pedaled uphill, focusing on one place in particular. Looking like it had seen many better days, the Petrie house lay nestled amongst the overgrown foliage sprouting up around it. The front lawn starkly contrasted with the neighbors' pristine yards laying on either side.

Pip could not shake the horrible feeling deep inside. The feeling that had been with him since the night before.

Coming to a stop, he decided he would not throw the paper onto the Petries' porch. Not today.

Letting his bike drop onto the long grass, Pip grabbed a paper from the hessian bag on his handlebars. With some trepidation, he walked up the stone path toward the front door. He felt like he was being pulled, compelled somehow to knock on the Petrie's door. His conscience would not let him ride by even if he wanted to.

The morning so far had felt like a dream, and Pip could not focus on anything. He needed to do something to appease his misguided guilt.

As his finger pressed on the doorbell, the chimes inside blared. Even the tune it played sounded melancholy.

His blood suddenly ran cold as he felt a pang of regret for what he was doing. He questioned why he was even there, as he gripped the paper tightly and began to turn around. *This isn't a good idea*, he thought.

Before he could step off the porch, the front door opened.

"Hello?" came a frail voice.

Looking over his shoulder, Pip saw the haggard woman standing in the doorway.

Adam Petrie's mother was only in her late forties but looked twenty years older at least. Her nightie was dirty and frayed. Her hair was unkempt and knotted. Her eyes were sunken as if she had not slept for weeks.

"Oh, hello you!" Her eyes lit up as she recognized Pip. "Is it the first of the month already? Let me get my purse."

As Mrs. Petrie turned, Pip spoke up. "No, please," he said. "I'm not here for the money. It's only the 11th today."

"It is?" Mrs. Petrie looked confused. "Well, how can I help you, young man? Is everything okay?"

"I..." Pip's words froze as he looked up at this woman. He remembered her dropping Adam off at school. How young and vibrant she seemed back then. But he had delivered her paper for the past couple of years and seen her looking sadder and sadder every time she opened the door to pay him. He remembered her much more than Adam. Adam was just another face in his class. Someone who didn't say or do much. But his mother was always loud and happy and made herself known. But not now.

"Yes?"

"I wanted," Pip forced the words out. "I just wanted to say I'm sorry. I should have said this a long time ago. But—"

"Sorry for what?" Mrs. Petrie asked, taking a step nearer to him. "Is everything okay?"

"Adam," Pip said quietly. "I'm sorry about Adam. I never said it before, and I should have. But I wanted to say now. I'm really sorry it all happened to you."

Mrs. Petrie's eyes opened wide. "Adam?" was all she could mutter.

"I was in his class," Pip continued, needing to explain himself. "And me and my friends remembered him yesterday, and I... I..." He stared down at his feet. "I just wanted to tell you I'm sorry for what you went through. I see you every month, and you look so sad, and I never said it before. I thought I—"

"My boy," Mrs. Petrie smiled. "I'm not sad."

Pip looked up at her. He did not know why but fought back tears that seemed to overcome him with no notice. It was as if he was feeling grief *for* her.

"You were in the same class with my Adam?" she said. "You were friends?"

"Yes," he lied. "We sat next to each other," he lied again. If questioned, he could not honestly say why he had lied. He simply felt like he had to.

"Pip, isn't it?" Without waiting for a reply, she continued. "He never mentioned you, but.." She smiled weakly as her gaze fell toward her feet. "It's all been a blur these past few years."

"I'm sorry, I shouldn't have bothered you," Pip said as he handed her the paper. But she didn't take it. Instead, she looked wistfully across the lawn.

"Friends," she muttered, happier by the moment. "Maybe that's what will bring him inside?"

Pip held the paper out higher, "I should go."

"You were *really* his friend?" Mrs. Petrie looked back down at him. "I had no idea he had any."

"Um," Pip had to lie again, but did so reluctantly. "Yeah. Very good friends."

"Well, in that case, I have something to show you. Something beautiful."

Before he could find the will to politely decline and

turn back, Pip was ushered inside the dusty, old house onto a ragged old rug in the hallway.

"I'm sorry," Pip said with some urgency. "I have to deliver the rest of the papers."

Mrs. Petrie shut the front door; the click of the lock unsettled his nerves.

"Nonsense," she said. "Your deliveries can wait."

As PIP OPENED HIS EYES, he felt a stinging on the back of his head.

He had no recollection of what had happened after he walked into the Petrie house. His mind scrambled as it searched for an explanation to it all. *Did I faint?* he thought to himself.

His eyes began to focus on an orange glow that was filling the room. His vision was blurry, and his head throbbed. The glow began to form into the large hanging light in the room.

Managing to turn his gaze down to his arms, he hazily noticed some rope tying his limbs to the oversized wooden chair he was sitting on.

Confused and frightened, Pip looked around the room. He could tell he was in a dining room. Against the far wall was his bike, propped next to an antique sideboard.

He was sat at the head of a large dining table. A plate of hot lasagna sat in front of him and two other vacant places.

At the far end of the room, in front of a pair of open curtainless sliding doors that overlooked the backyard, stood Mrs. Petrie, her back to him, staring out. No longer bedraggled in her nightie, she wore a finely pressed dress.

Her hair was brushed and tied up in a neat bun. A chilly breeze from outside wafted in and filled the room.

Pip noticed how dark it was outside, almost too dark. He tried to speak, but he realized tape was covering his mouth. He managed to make a panicked, yet muffled, yelp.

Mrs. Petrie turned and saw his anguish. She smiled. "Oh, my dear boy, I'm sorry. But I *had* to do all this." She motioned to the chair he was tied to. "I want you here for dinner. It's good to have a friend of Adam's here. You would have called me mad if I had just asked you." She turned back to glance outside. "It's so nice. So very nice."

Pip yelled with all his might, but the tape muffled the sound.

In the hallway outside, the grandfather clock rang out.

Pip turned toward the chimes.

He instinctively counted. He felt a need to know the time.

When it got past nine *bongs* of the clock, Pip's mind raced. *Nine? Is it after nine? They must be worried sick about me.*

But the chimes did not stop there. When they reached twelve, Mrs. Petrie turned to him joyously.

"My dear boy." She said as she walked over from the open door and sat in a chair next to him, "It's time. They come here every night, and I open the door... But they won't come in... I've begged them... But tonight... tonight is *special*. You're *special*. You *have* to be the key!"

She turned and stared out into the darkness of the yard and the woodland beyond.

"He must have missed you so," she whispered. "*Finally,* he can have a friend."

Pip could not concentrate as he tried to will the pain in

his head to disappear. The throbbing seared through his skull as if trying to warn him the only way it could. If his pain had a voice to speak, it would be screaming as loudly as it could; *RUN, RUN, RUUUUUUN.*

"He's *here*," she said in tears. "My baby Adam... My darling..."

Those were not the words that stole Pip's attention. It was the following sentence that caused his head to jolt up, and force him to focus on something besides his panic.

"Bixley!" she exclaimed. "They both look so happy to see you!"

He pushed his pain into the background as much as he could, as his eyes strained to fight the blurry vision approaching him. Pip could see shapes coming out of the darkness, along the floor. *He swore he could see branches.*

As the yellow mist seeped in the open door, made its way across the table, and encircled his bound feet, a new shape stepped inside. As it hit the light, the mist that swirled thickly around Pip cleared.

It was Adam and Bixley. Walking into the kitchen at a very slow pace.

Adam was dressed in filthy ripped clothes and not looking a day older than when he died. His pale eyes had locked on Pip. Bixley, meanwhile, mimicked his master's actions; moving slowly and not looking anywhere else except straight at Pip, with an almost identical wide smile. A wide, overly toothy smile. Wide, yet absolutely terrifying.

Pip's muffled screams made little difference. His palpable terror made the boy's ghostly figure grin further as it approached.

"They've never looked so happy," Mrs. Petrie said, leaping to her feet. "Come in! My beautiful boy. Please come in! Look, Adam, it's your friend! We can be a family again, yes? Say we can be! Finally!"

As Pip uttered a strangled scream, his eyes filled with horror-stricken tears at the grinning figures now uncomfortably close.

Approaching as if on rails, neither Adam nor Bixley's legs moved as they walked, but somehow they still advanced through the mist. Their attention was now all focused on Pip. They were *only* focused on Pip. Their smiles grew impossibly wider as they drew nearer. Nearer. Nearer.

"Sit!" Mrs. Petrie implored. "Eat!"

But they did not sit.

She ran in front of Adam and knelt to hug him. But he continued ignoring her embrace, not once turning back. Showing zero interest in her presence or pleading.

"Adam?" She weakly whimpered as her son moved away. "It's me. Mommy. Please. *Take me too!*"

But Adam did not answer her.

Realizing the futility of her plight, Mrs. Petrie wailed, collapsing in a flood of tears.

Adam and Bixley moved in unison closer and closer to Pip. Snaking over to him through the thick yellow mist.

Closer and closer.

ACROSS TOWN, the voices of Reverend Philip Kaminsky and his wife Sarah rang loudly as they called Pip's name, walking through the streets. Many other parents and children had joined the search, all desperately calling out to Pip.

Emmie, James, Findley, and Hamish were there too.

They stood together, sharing a look of terror. Arthur, the Great Dane, was held on a leash in James' hand, walking obediently by its small owner's side.

Though they could not explain why—each of them knew deep inside that this search would turn out to be fruitless, even if they would never admit such a sad thought aloud. They each felt the similar sinking in their stomachs, something that told them that Pip was far from okay.

ADAM APPROACHED PIP, his jaw seemingly unhinged. His teeth gleamed with a thick viscous drool. At his feet, Bixley grinned the same kind of grin, dripping with the same kind of drool. His eyes filled with the *same* type of hunger.

They may not have sat at the dining room table, but they *did* eat.

DENIAL & DISCOVERY

The police station felt like a principal's office to James. And just like whenever he was in his principal's office, he had burst into tears at least half a dozen times during the sheriff's questioning. Now sitting on a plastic chair outside the interview room, next to his parents, he could not stop thinking about what had been asked; about Pip having run away. That he must say if he knew *anything*. But James did not, and the floods of tears told them as much.

"It's okay, baby," his mom, Kathy, said as she cuddled him from the next seat. "I know this is horrible for you, for *everyone*. It'll all be okay. I'm sure of it."

"P—Pip will be okay too, right?" James asked.

Kathy just smiled in reply.

"He will, won't he?" James asked again, this time with more urgency in his voice. "They'll find him soon?"

Kathy looked over to her husband, Binh, sitting on a chair against the other side of the corridor. She smiled, silently urging him to help.

Getting the message, Binh leaned forward to his son. "James," he said softly.

James looked up and wiped tears from his cheeks with the cuff of his sweater.

"We don't know if Pip will be okay, but whatever happens, your mom and I will protect you." He searched for the right words. "I hope this is all nothing. We *all* do. And the police will do all they can, I promise."

James did not reply; he merely looked down

sorrowfully and then closed his eyes. Binh shrugged at Kathy, a silent gesture to say that at least he tried.

Shouting from inside the interview room behind them broke the silence.

"No," Findley yelled at Sheriff Matt Benson from the other side of the metal table.

Amber Scott could not find words fast enough. She was shocked at her son for shouting at a policeman, but it did not surprise her. Her son was prone to giving in to his emotions in times of stress at home, but she never expected the same here.

"How *dare* you," Findley pointed his finger at the Sheriff, "Take it back!"

"I'm so sorry," Amber said to Matt. "He didn't mean—"

"Oh, I meant it all right!" Findley interrupted. "Pip did *not* do anythin' you're saying. He would *never* do it. Never."

"Please, calm down," Matt said, his palms outward to diffuse the situation.

"You think he *stole money*?!" Findley almost spat in anger. "You know *nothing* about Pip!"

The fact this policeman was in a position of authority meant nothing to Findley. The fact that he was scarcely a quarter of the Sheriff's age meant nothing to Findley. All that mattered to Findley was the truth.

"Fin," Amber pleaded to her son. "Baby. No one is lying."

"Mrs. Petrie paid him the money. We know it," Matt said, shrugging. "Then he disappeared. I don't know what more proof you need that your friend—"

"You said Pip told her she had to pay him for a year's worth of papers, right?" Findley asked, still pointing at the policeman. "So, why didn't she get a receipt? Whenever you pay the paper bill, Pip gives those little paper notes. Always. Where is it? Huh?"

Matt didn't answer.

"I *bet* she didn't have one," Findley continued. "And what, two hundred bucks? Where would it get him?"

Through the glass in the door, Findley spotted Mrs. Petrie walking past, accompanied by another policeman. Findley leaped to his feet and followed them.

"We haven't finished here, son," Matt stated in a loud stern voice.

"Findley!" Amber said again in shock.

Opening the door to the interview room, Findley stormed out, walked past James and his parents, and strode down the hall after Mrs. Petrie, who was now standing by the exit, held open by the police officer.

"You're a stinkin' liar, Mrs. Petrie!" Findley shouted after her.

With shock, Mrs. Petrie turned and stared wide-eyed at her accuser.

"You tell them all," Findley continued, his voice now louder. "You tell them Pip did *not* take your money. Liar!"

"Get back here!" the Sheriff commanded as he strode out of the room after him.

The whole Tran family could only look on helplessly at what was happening around them.

"*Liar!*" Findley repeated as Matt grabbed his arm and dragged him back to the room. "*Liar! Liar! Liar!*"

Before he lost sight of Mrs. Petrie, he saw her turn, a smile cracking her face—a cruel and victorious smile.

. . .

THERE WOULD BE no funeral for Philip 'Pip' Kaminsky Jr. No obituaries were written. No body was found. No trace of anything. All the police and the townsfolk could piece together was, according to his parents, Pip had seemed very depressed that night. Then, the following day, Pip had told both of them he loved them, then gave them each a big hug —which was slightly out of character for someone so shy and reserved. He then left on his bike to deliver his newspapers.

His bike had been found leaning against a building near the train tracks, along with the undelivered papers.

The working theory was the boy had tricked Mrs. Petrie into giving him money, which he used to run away—getting on the train and leaving without a word.

"IT'S ALL BILLSHUT!" Findley exclaimed with a standard invented obscenity as he stared out the window. "No way he'd take her money and run! Not him!"

"Calm down," Emmie pleaded as she stood up from the clubhouse floor and walked over to her friend. Placing her hand on his shoulder, she turned him to face her. "We are *all* on the same side. None of us believes that he'd run away, right?" She turned her question to Hamish and James, sitting on the floor next to each other.

"Yeah," Hamish agreed. "Not him."

James simply nodded along. Not knowing what he could or should say.

Findley, meanwhile, got more visibly upset. "You didn't see her face."

"And you're *sure* it was a smile?" Hamish asked. "Some people look like they are smiling when they cry. Like this..."

His face contorted with exaggerated grief, his mouth wide and showing his teeth like a twisted smile.

"It *was* a smile," Findley said, his voice mournful. "One hundred and fifty percent."

"Okay, let's say that she *did* smile at Fin," Emmie said, taking charge of the conversation. "Let's say that she knows what happened to Pip."

Findley nodded. "That's what I'm saying. I've—"

"—Right," Emmie cut in. "Now let's say all that is true. What do we do? What *can* we do? We can't just turn up at her house and ask, can we? She'll just lie again."

No one replied.

"See?" Emmie continued. "She didn't tell the police; she won't just tell us. Besides, if she is the one who did something to Pip, it's too risky."

"You think she kidnapped him?" Hamish asked timidly. "To be her new Adam or something?"

Emmie shrugged. "She's at least gotta know what happened."

"Guys," James changed tack, "Pip had a diary, right? The one he was always writing something in."

"Yeah," Hamish replied.

"If he ran away, wouldn't he have taken it?" James asked.

"Yeah, exactly," Findley replied, thinking aloud, and sounding almost surprised at his conclusions.

"And?" Emmie did not know where this was going.

"And if he *didn't* run away, it would be in his room, right?" James beamed. "In his school bag? He wouldn't take it on his route."

"He would have written in it the night before he disappeared!" Emmie caught on.

"If it's there, we know for *sure* he didn't run," Findley smiled.

"He may have written in there if someone was following him or something, yeah?" Hamish joined in.

James nodded. "Might be in his bag and that would give us a clue!"

"And if it's not there," Emmie said, turning toward Findley seriously. "Even though it sucks, we gotta at least *consider* that he did run away. And that *maybe* Mrs. Petrie didn't smile at you, and it was... crying... or something."

"The diary'll be there," Findley stated with absolute certainty. "I just know it."

"So," a confused Hamish said, "how do we find out if he took it?"

For a few seconds, they fell silent. Each deep in thought, until James smirked, let out a small chuckle, then clicked his fingers.

"Easy," James said victoriously. "Pip never locks his window."

As the cold night set in, James, Findley, Hamish, and Emmie snuck out of their respective homes, having been told categorically by their parents that they were not allowed out past dark. Though Pip was a presumed runaway, neither parent nor authority took any chances. Neither their parents nor the authorities wanted to take any chances. An informal curfew was put into effect.

Kristofer and Simon Flynn peered into Hamish's dark bedroom. As they saw the shadowy lump under the covers, they felt relief and then shut the door as quietly as possible.

They had no idea that under those covers were piles of their son's clothes.

A similar scene played out in James and Findley's houses, with them pretending to be asleep in their room. Only Emmie strolled out of her house without even trying to be quiet, slamming the door behind her. Heath Hanson, her father, was out until late, as he always seemed to be. He often left Emmie to feed and look after herself. While Emmie's mother was alive, his job as manager and owner of *Heath Hanson Motors* never kept him away from home beyond 6 pm. It was his business after all, and he had final say on his working hours. Now though, since her passing, he buried himself so deep in his job, that he rarely returned before midnight. He did not even know about Pip's disappearance or the police questioning his daughter. When the police said a parent or guardian must be present, Emmie requested Hamish's father be there instead. Though not strictly legal, Sheriff Benson allowed it, as he knew the Hanson family well. He had been friends with Emmie's mother and now knew the girl was often left to her own devices through her father's grief-stricken neglect.

"I don't like this one bit," James whispered to Hamish as they stood at the base of the tree at the back of the Kaminsky home.

Hamish didn't answer, but he felt the same sense of dread as James. Standing in the thick shadows was terrible enough, but being a party to a breaking and entering was much worse.

Looking up, the boys stared as Emmie and Findley crawled across the thick branch leading up to Pip's unlocked bedroom window. Sliding it open with ease, they then crept inside without making a sound.

"I'm sure his mom and dad would have let us in to look for the diary if we asked," James pondered aloud. "They want to find him, too, right?"

Hamish blew on his hands to warm them up, then shrugged. "No turning back now," he said as he motioned to the window his friends had just climbed through. "When those two get a thought in their head, it's hard to get 'em to do anything else."

STANDING in the darkness of Pip's room, Findley stepped cautiously across the carpet to where Pip's school bag hung from the post at the foot of his bed.

"Jackpot," he muttered louder than intended as he reached for the bag.

"*Shhhhh,*" Emmie hushed him in a panic.

Immediately filling with dread, he paused as his hand touched the edge of the strap. Not wanting to move a muscle in case anyone heard him.

Both remained quiet for a few seconds, listening intently for any sign that they had been discovered.

They had seen Pip's parents through the dining room window only a few minutes earlier, sitting at the table and looking distraught as they spoke. They held each other's hands across the table comfortingly, both talking with tears in their eyes.

"I think it's safe," Emmie whispered.

Nodding, Findley then grasped the bag's strap and lifted it gently off the bedpost, moving it onto the bed, where he sat without causing a single squeak from the mattress springs.

He stared at the zipped-up rucksack on his lap, hesitant

to open it for fear of finding the journal missing. Because if the journal was indeed not there, then it would mean that Pip did run away. And if that were the case, it would also mean that none of his friends knew Pip well enough to see the truth or help him if he was troubled.

Emmie tiptoed across the carpet and over to the bed, then sat beside Findley.

"It's gonna be okay," was all she needed to say.

Findley nodded, then unzipped the bag, careful to make no noise.

"HURRY THE HELL UP," James muttered as he looked around. Meanwhile, Hamish stared upward and did not notice the fear now creeping over his friend. The backyard they hid in was now bathed in thick black shadow. Shadows that seemed *too* dark to be natural.

James shivered as he looked at this thick, inky blackness surrounding them.

"They gotta hurry!" He turned to Hamish, beginning to feel quite frantic. "Hamish, they really—"

"They took him!" came a raised and distraught voice from inside the house, stealing both boys' attention away from their thoughts.

IN PIP'S BEDROOM, Findley had not yet looked in the bag as he and Emmie heard Sarah Kaminsky's angry and upset words from downstairs.

"I'm telling you; those woods took our boy!"

Nodding her head toward the door, Emmie stood from

the bed. Gingerly and quietly, she moved closer. Findley, with Pip's bag in hand, quickly joined her.

Emmie nervously grabbed the door handle.

"Quietly," Findley urged.

The Reverend's voice was heard replying to his wife in a much calmer and quieter tone. "Please, Sarah, you're not thinking clearly."

As the bedroom door cracked open without a sound, both Findley and Emmie peered out into the hallway. The downstairs voices of Pip's parents then became a lot clearer.

"You *know* what happened to me!" Sarah said, sounding like she was about to burst into wails of tears. "It was that *thing* in those woods! It's happening again. There's no other explanation."

"The police said—" The Reverend began but was immediately cut off.

"Screw the police! Matt Benson knows *exactly* how dangerous those woods are. He's just scared... like he's always been."

"You were all *children*," her husband said, his tone too sensible for her liking. "You can't be *sure* what you saw. I mean, come on... Monsters in the trees?"

"Me, him, Mikey Fisk, Gerry Levy, we *all* saw it, right there in the dead woods! We didn't imagine it!"

Philip held her hands across the table, trying to support her, regretting trying to impose his own logic onto her.

Just as Findley was about to retreat into the room, Pip's mother said something that filled him and Emmie with fear—freezing them to the spot.

"He covered up what happened to us exactly like he did that poor Petrie boy's murder. He was too scared, simple as that." Sarah's voice was starting to crack with upset. "He lied and said I was wrong after I tried to tell everyone the truth... About those marks all over that boy's body, like he lied when we lost Gerry. He didn't want to face the truth of any of it... I saw that boy's body when we had to bury him. It was eaten! It looked like fang marks all over him, and Matt made me doubt myself *again*. But not now. No way."

Findley and Emmie glanced at each other, not knowing what to think or say.

"What does this have to do with Pip?" the Reverend asked.

"It *has* to all be linked," she shouted. "How did I not see it til today? I allowed Matt to convince me it was all my imagination." Her voice fell to a whisper as she spoke. "But it wasn't, was it? I saw a monster in those woods. I saw the bites on the poor boy... Now Pip last seen where that boy died? No one can explain a thing, and are telling lies about what happened. Covering all three things up. They *have* to be linked. Just have to be"

"Sarah," the reverend said, as though saying her name might calm her, bring her back to reason. But it did not.

She believed with all her being that she was right, no matter how insane it all sounded, yet he had to try. "People live by Cromwell Woods, and kids have played in them for years. If it were so dangerous, wouldn't everyone have seen the things by now? Wouldn't more people have gone missing? You're forcing a link where there is none."

"Those woods have our Pip." Upon saying his name, she burst out sobbing. "I thought it was gone. I thought what we saw must have left or died after it took Gerry... Then that boy, that poor boy... And now Pip. Right in the same place. I didn't know the Petrie house was by those woods until today. I never thought of looking at the address when he came in. I merely work with the bodies. I don't go to the scene. But in the same place where Pip went missing? Right by the woods? Where that boy lived? Right by the woods... How else could anyone explain it? The boy died from bites from something. I saw them. I saw the size of them. But there was no trace of an animal anywhere. And then they found his dog dead; I *know* it had the same size teeth. Even if I couldn't prove it, I just knew."

"Please, Sarah," he implored again. "You're tired. You're making no sense."

"I'm telling you, it wasn't natural," she said, ignoring his comment. "It's all *super*natural. The same as what I saw back then. And now... Now our baby... And Matt's telling us he's a thief and ran away? He's lying again. This can't be a coincidence. It can't be. It's a pattern. And that Petrie woman *knows* what happened!"

"I'm sorry, I don't see the link you do. I just want to—"

"If I thought that thing in the woods was still there," Sarah interrupted. "I'd never have let Pip go near that part of town... Not if I saw this link... Never... I would have moved us somewhere safe. But I thought it was gone. I didn't see the truth of any of it all until now."

Then there was a long pause, broken only by the sobbing of both parents.

"We need sleep," the Reverend eventually said as he sniffed away his runny nose. "We can see Matt in the morning, okay? If not, we'll confront that Petrie woman ourselves. Forgetting monsters, her saying our Pip stole her money... I can't accept that. I just can't."

Findley felt a hand on his shoulder. Turning, he saw Emmie motion him back to the open window.

"C'mon, we gotta go," she whispered with some urgency. "Before they come upstairs and find us."

"WHAT HAPPENED?" James asked Findley as they walked down the middle of the deserted street, the lights on either side of the asphalt illuminating their path home.

Findley and Emmie walked wide-eyed and in silence. They did not know what to think after what they had heard.

"Don't leave us in suspense." Hamish said as he tapped the rucksack slung over Findley's shoulder. "What you got in the bag?"

Turning her head, Emmie looked shocked as she noticed the rucksack Findley carried. "Oh damn, you took it?"

Obliviously, Findley turned his gaze to the bag on his shoulder. With sudden realization, he broke out in a cold sweat. "I... I didn't think."

Without another moment passing, he slung the bag down to the road and unzipped it. As the fabric of the top of the rucksack parted, a small bright gold journal appeared atop some of Pip's school books.

"Bingo!" James said with a smile as he noticed the journal. "He didn't run!"

Findley turned to Emmie with a look of dread, then back at Hamish and James. "I wish he did," he said. "I really do."

"What d'ya mean?" Hamish asked.

"Was it to do with all that shouting?" James asked.

Emmie nodded. "You hear that?"

"Not a lot," James replied and shook his head. "Could only hear shouting, not what they said."

They stared at each other for a few uncomfortable moments.

"Well?" Hamish prompted. "We gotta guess or what?"

"It's bad," Findley said.

"What's bad?" Hamish asked as he turned to Emmie, hoping for more clarity.

"It's real, real bad," Emmie added.

In the dull street light, the four trudged their way home, Emmie and Findley retelling what they had heard about that *thing* in Cromwell Woods—the dead woods—whatever that name meant.

THE TREE MAN

1968

Lying to the north of the town, Cromwell Woods was not a place many people went to for fun, as long-dead trees populated the area, and anyone going there was in danger of getting in the way of a falling tree—which happened more often than it should. That did not stop children, though, as they ventured in to play amongst the large and parentless expanse of deceased woodland. Though, as night came, and the mists filled the woodland floor, anyone in there quickly ran away, terrified at what they imagined could be hiding and waiting to pounce. As far back as anyone can remember, the town council at Hemlock Creek had planned to level the woods and build on the land. Still, any ideas were summarily dismissed whenever the costs involved were realized. Then the woods were left alone again, abandoned in the hope that some investor may one day come along and see the potential in the dry land.

"It looks like a face, dunnit?" Mikey Fisk asked no one in particular as he stared up at the collection of entwining dead branches high up in the trees in front of them. "Kinda looking down on us, smilin'. Like it's happy we're here."

"Shut up, Mikey," Gerry Levy said, kneeling in the center of a clearing, the lack of vegetation there suggesting the earth had spoiled. A pile of leaves and twigs lay in front of him as he busily worked on a fire plow he had quickly assembled. Rubbing two sticks frantically together, he tried to create a spark. "No one wants to know about your stupid tree people!"

Mike turned toward his friends, all fifteen and all Sophomores. Best friends, should anyone ask.

With the dark quickly approaching, the dulled daylight threw a fairy-tale glow over the area, making it seem like a fantastical and dream-like place. The clearing they were in was almost perfectly circular, with some fallen trees lying across the middle as if nature had made for them a rustic campsite.

"I see a face," Sarah Charles said, looking up at where Mikey had been staring. "It really does look like it's smiling, right?"

"I never see stuff like that," Matt Benson said as he reached into his pocket and brought out a pack of gum. "Like looking at clouds. Everyone sees dogs, people or boats, or whatever. You know what I see?"

"Clouds?" Gerry replied, still frantically rubbing the sticks together.

Matt clapped his hands, then pointed to Gerry, "You get an A. Go to the head of the class, *and* you win the Superbowl. You are *exactly* right.... Goddamn clouds! That's all. Stupid, stupid clouds."

"Tree man is going to judge you harshly for doubting his existence," Mikey said with a smile. "Right, tree man?" He chuckled as he sat on the ground opposite the fallen tree, where Matt and Sarah were sitting.

They all turned their attention toward the face in the pattern of crossed branches above them.

"Yes, Mikey, you are right," Mikey said in a comically gruff voice. The voice of his invented Tree Man. "I am well and truly pissed off at you, Matthew."

The group laughed as Gerry snorted loudly in amusement, without any pause in his attempts to start a fire.

"Ah, the piggie is amused," Mikey said, carrying on his Tree Man impression.

This caused Gerry to snort in laughter even louder.

Matthew snorted, too, for comedic mockery, as did Sarah.

Soon all three of them sounded like a group of piglets.

"Fools, the lot of you!" Mikey continued his impression. "Tree man is *furious*."

The snorts gave way to laughter as the daylight faded.

With the clearing getting darker and darker by the second, they did not notice the thin yellow mist crawling over the dirt ground and wafting innocuously around them.

"We really gotta get back," Matt said as the laughter died out. He looked around at the lengthening shadows. "If piglet here can't get a fire goin', I don't wanna be sat in the middle of this place in the dark."

Sarah leaned into him, snuggling her head against his neck. "I'll protect you from Tree Man, don't you worry."

Matt wrapped his arm around her and kissed her on the forehead. "Thanks, babe," he said. "I need all the protection I can get."

Mikey reached into his pocket, brought out his wallet—held together with string—grabbed a condom from its side, then tossed the crumpled packet over to Matt, who easily caught it.

Realizing what the thrown packet contained, Sarah burst out laughing. "Well, you *asked* for protection," she said to Matt.

"I'll put it to good use," Matt quipped, pocketing the condom.

"Hey, I was joking," Mikey complained. "Give it back!"

Gerry paused from his fire-making, and glanced at Mikey. "And you'll do what with it, exactly, Mr. Fisk?" he asked cockily. "Use it to carry your books to school?"

"Hey, I could get any guy I wanted, you know?" Mikey retorted as he looked up at the smiling face he had seen in the trees, now blending in with the darkness. The face was now faded in the darkness. Adopting his deep impression of Tree Man, Mikey said. "I like you, Mikey. Let's do it!" His normal voice resumed. "Aw, thank you, Tree Man. I hope you don't give me splinters in my ass!"

The group all burst out laughing again.

"Cute," Matt said. He then patted his jacket pocket. "But I'm still keeping this!"

Mikey shrugged as he laughed. "Ah well, it was worth the joke."

"And now, I can honestly say," Gerry said as he sat back and regarded his failed fire-making attempt in front of him, "I have zero ideas of what I am doing."

"What the hell? You've been at this for ages," Sarah said. "You said you could make a fire!"

"Ah, I can," Gerry said as he pulled a lighter from his jeans pocket. "Just not with those damn twigs." Flicking the lighter on, Gerry then lowered the flame into the collection of dry leaves and twigs. In an instant, fire engulfed the kindling.

Matt guffawed, finding it all hilarious. "You had a lighter all along? Bravo, my friend. Bravo!"

Mikey looked dramatically shocked as he playacted his reaction. "Fire? In the dead woods? You know who'll be angry?" His eyes darted around in fear, as if scared of who was around. "You know who'll want revenge for you burning his dead leaf children?"

Sarah laughed. "Don't tell us," she said, turning to Gerry and Matt.

"Tree Man!" The group exclaimed in unison.

At that moment, they all turned to look up at the face in the trees.

Now illuminated by the approaching moonlight, the face they had seen in the trees no longer smiled; instead, it looked angry, with a furrowed brow and a grimacing mouth.

Even though Matt could not see the happy Tree Man's face before, he clearly saw the angry face hanging amongst the trees.

Their laughter quickly stopped as they looked wide-eyed at the contorted face within the dead branches.

Without averting his gaze, Gerry got to his feet and patted out the fire with his shoe. "I think it's time we get the hell out of here. You all good with that, yeah?"

"Yup," Mikey said as he stood up. "Let's skedaddle."

Before Matt and Sarah could move, Gerry was suddenly yanked backward. Something unseen had ripped him from where he stood and pulled him off his feet and away from the clearing, into the darkness of the tree line.

He barely had time to scream. He could only yelp, but all sound was soon silenced by the darkness engulfing him.

Matt, Sarah, and Mikey had no time to stop what had happened. They all screamed as soon as they witnessed this impossible attack on Gerry.

"Gerry!" Mikey gasped as he scrambled after where his friend had disappeared. But as soon as he got to the tree line, like two magnets colliding, his body felt an enormous shock, the force repelling him to the ground.

"No!" Sarah yelled as Matt sprang to his feet and picked Mikey off the floor.

Sarah then turned back to the face in the trees for reasons she did not know.

Looking down at her, the wooden visage was now somehow angrier.

Sarah's mind reeled as she tried to understand everything.

"*Gerry!*" Mikey bellowed into the darkness in front of him.

Sarah's eyes then moved to the surrounding foliage, specifically the shadows within them.

Her blood soon ran cold.

"Matt," she muttered, frantically pointing at the tree line. "Look!"

Barely able to think straight, Matt turned and saw where she was pointing: a shadow in the tree line resembled the shape of a person. A large, cloaked person.

"*Gerrrrrrrry!*" Mikey continued screaming, unaware of the new dangers Sarah and Matt saw.

They stood speechless, staring at the shadow. Both of them knew this was something more than simple darkness playing a trick on their eyes.

Turning to Mikey, Matt then caught sight of another shadow at the other side of the clearing—another large human shape.

With the darkness now settled in for the night, the sun's glow was but a memory. The moonlight had crept in and replaced it with its weak glare, failing to do much to these woods aside from making every shadow look more threatening.

None of them noticed the yellow mist getting thicker and thicker.

"What do we do?" Mikey said in a tearful panic as he turned to Matt.

But Matt was too busy staring at the shadows around him, filled with fear, distracted, and afraid to reply rationally.

Sarah then broke down, collapsing to the dirt in tears.

Matt could only stare at the shadows as a cold fear consumed him.

Mikey shouted toward the woods. "Gerry!"

"No need to shout, Michael," came a voice from the shadows. A familiar voice. But one that sounded eerily calm and monotone.

Mikey directed his attention to a large shadow looming over them between the trees. "What the hell?" he said, his confusion and upset entwining into an almost debilitating frenzy.

Looking into the shadow, Sarah recognized the voice. "Gerry?" She asked through her tears. "Is that you?"

"Yes," replied the shadow.

Matt, though was not tearful. Instead, he felt a rage growing inside of him. "What the hell, Gerry?" he exclaimed in anger as he strode over to the shadow at the tree line. "What the hell was that? How did you—" His words faded as he got to where the shadow figure had been. Where the darkness thinned, and the shadow got brighter until it disappeared.

"Why did you do that?" Sarah pleaded from behind, still seeing the shadow right next to where Matt now stood.

"Do not fear," the same voice said again, but now from the other side of the clearing. They all turned and saw another human-looking shadow between the dead tree stumps.

"*What're you doin'?*" Mikey shouted. "*What the hell's goin' on?*"

A face appeared as the shadow moved forward from the darkness. It was Gerry or something that looked identical to him. This Gerry, though, was significantly paler. Deathly paler. His skin was so gray it was almost translucent in the moonlight. His eyes had lost all color.

As the three others silently watched their friend staring right back at them, they felt a primordial fear grip them tightly.

This haunting Gerry merely smiled.

Almost instinctively, Sarah glanced around at the Tree Man in the branches, whose expression had turned from happy, to angry, to even angrier. Now it stared down at her with a devilishly cruel expression. The branches making up the pattern of the face now seemed to have multiplied. Where before it was a crude shape discernible only by those with imagination, now was heavily detailed with a multitude its wooden limbs. The visage staring down at her went beyond a simple shape of eyes and a mouth. It now showed angry eyebrows and rows of sharp, pointed teeth— each made from the smallest of dead branches.

Gerry's smile grew.

"Please, stop messin' around like this," Mikey pleaded.

Gerry's smile grew wider.

And wider.

"Please—" Mikey stopped pleading as he realized this wasn't his friend.

As the smile grew and grew, reaching further and further across his cheeks, this Gerry's eyes began to pale and glow a milky yellowish hue. His once happy, brown eyes now gave way to this supernatural glow. This thing then opened its mouth, stretching the width of its head. It levered backward as if on a hinge. From this vast gaping maw, vines then spouted out. Long black thorny vines. They all crept out of this Gerry's mouth and beckoningly reached out toward his friends.

"Run!" Matt yelped, spinning around and picking up Sarah, who had lay on the dirt, incapacitated from fear.

"Mikey! RUN!" Matt screamed again as he bolted from the clearing, back in the direction of home. Away from whatever it was they were seeing.

In a blind panic, Matt sprinted as fast as he could. Sarah gripped him as he held her in his arms. Though she was not a small person, Matt's adrenaline pumped through his body so forcefully he could barely notice her weight in his arms. He focused only on running; if he gave in to anything else, he thought he would not make it.

"Mikey," he shouted back over his shoulder. "Come on!"

The subsequent minutes went by in a terrifying blur. Sarah had her eyes shut tight as Matt carried her. She blocked out everything she could as she prayed to herself for the safe confines of her bed. Meanwhile, Matt raced through the trees as fast as he could, ignoring the shadows around him.

Matt did not know *when* he got out of the woods. When his panic eventually subsided and his mind grasped the ability to focus, he realized that he was standing at the corner of Oliver Street and Medway—the main junction in the center of Hemlock Creek. He still carried a terrified

Sarah in his arms as he looked around at the townspeople —those out for an evening meal, as well as those on their way home from a late shift. No one at first noticed either of them, bloodied and battered in the middle of the road.

"Someone, anyone... Help us!" Matt shouted with all his might as the exhaustion finally caught up with him, and he collapsed to the asphalt, right in the middle of the road, still cradling Sarah.

THE FEEDBACK from the microphone reverberated around the town hall in a painful squeal as Sheriff Eddis Eaves-Eagleton tapped on it. The audience winced in audible pain.

"Sorry," he mumbled, his voice blaring over the speakers. "I can't work these God-finagling doodads." His tone matched his stern features. Aged in his late fifties, this man was trim and muscular. He wore a police uniform. One that was slightly too tight for him, but for a man in his peak condition, it suited him to the ground. Contrary to this youthful and healthy body, his face was weathered like old boot leather. Framing his chin was a long white beard.

"Agnes?" He called off-stage right as the microphone volume was turned down. Then his face lit up. "Ah," he said. "There we go. My beautiful Agnes saves the day again."

"Get on with it, E!" came a woman's voice from offstage.

"Yes, my dear." The Sheriff sighed with a smile.

Some in the audience chuckled. But this was not the meeting where there should be any levity. Those people who had laughed immediately muted themselves as they realized where and why they were there.

The Sheriff's smile also fell away as he took a deep breath and looked out into the faces of the worried crowd. "Anyway, thanks for coming out tonight, folks. I know you're all as anxious to get answers as anyone. Well, I'm here to address all those concerns for you the best I can."

The crowd of nearly two hundred residents sat facing the podium with bated breath.

"For those who don't know me, I'm Sheriff Eaves-Eagleton. E. Those who know me know I'm not one to partake in gossip, or entertain anything less than complete honesty in the way I speak. And I bring that ethic here to you good people tonight." His eyes scanned the crowd until it rested on two people. A couple aged in their late thirties, both tired and frantic, gripped each other's hands tightly. "Mr. and Mrs. Levy, I appreciate you coming out at this tough time. You know all I'm going to say, so thank you for being with us tonight."

"What happened?" someone in the back asked.

"Hold yer horses. I'll get to it," the Sheriff said in annoyance as he raised his hand to them. "I know you need answers—"

"Are our kids safe?" asked another.

"Please," the Sheriff implored, but was interrupted again almost immediately.

"Those kids did it, didn't they?"

The Sheriff's polite demeanor faded as his voice turned loud and angry. "Shut your mouths, now!" He glared around the room. "You all better start showin' some *goddamn* respect!"

The audience had fallen silent, except for the sound of one person crying.

The Sheriff glanced down to the right of the crowd and

saw Sarah Charles in tears, held in her father's arms. "I'm sorry, Sarah," E said calmly. A tone that immediately switched back to anger as he addressed the people. "Next person to speak out of turn will be thrown out. And the next P.O.S. to make an innocent kid cry, you'll spend a week in my jail cell. You get me?"

No one dared reply.

"Now, no. 'The kids,' as you call 'em, didn't do squat." The Sheriff took a breath and bit his lip, gathering his thoughts. "Now, as you know, Matthew Benson and Sarah Charles were found in the town on the night of the 13th. The whereabouts of their friends, Michael Fisk and Gerald Levy, were unknown. We launched a search into the Cromwell woodland area. Some of you fine people were there helping us, which we are always grateful for." He took a deep breath before continuing. "As you know, we found the Fisk boy in the same area where he was last seen." He narrowed his eyes at the crowd. "Now I've heard all the B.S. about satanic rituals and other flights of fantasy y'all cooked up. I'm here to tell ya it is *all* lies. *All of it.* The poor Fisk boy was attacked by an animal. Those are the facts. He sustained significant injuries. All caused by sharp animal teeth and claws. So, any rumors you heard, just forget 'em."

"Which animal was it?" came a voice from the crowd.

The Sheriff's head shot up in the direction of where the voice came, straight at Neil Greatrix, one of the farmers from the outskirts of town.

With a wave of his hand, the Sheriff pointed to the farmer. "Get out before I throw you out," he shouted down the microphone.

"You can't do that," Greatrix said as his expression fell into confusion. "We got a right to ask questions."

"Boys?" the Sheriff shouted at his deputies at the back of the room. "Get him out, now."

In the few moments it took for the farmer to be escorted out of the hall, the Sheriff spent the whole time staring, in turn, at each person in the audience.

As the doors to the hall closed shut again, E continued.

"You know the rules. Keep your mouths shut 'til I'm done." Grabbing the small cup of water on the podium, the Sheriff took a sip and continued. "We confirmed it was an animal attack. However, we can't be sure which animal, as the beast didn't leave enough evidence for us to narrow it down. But whatever it was, it had a huge set of teeth." He looked down at the Levys and smiled sorrowfully, saying, "We can only assume the animal took Gerald. We haven't found any remains yet, so we can keep hope alive by keepin' on lookin'. So, for now, the Cromwell Woods are off-limits to all except authorized personnel. We got animal trackers coming down from Madison, and we've hired some of the best hunters in the county. But—and I can't believe I have to say this—anymore hoo-hah about devil worship, blood pacts, or ghosts in the woods, *anything* except this being a tragic event no one could foresee, then I'll show you the inside of a cell. If I hear *any* of you fine people even make a *single* whispered comment about this, and it *ain't* the truth? Well, as I just told ya, I'll... Well, let's say I won't be best pleased. Understand? Am I being crystal clear enough?"

The audience nodded or only stared back in shock.

The Sheriff then looked back at Sarah Charles. "You okay, Sarah?"

Though still with tear-streaked cheeks, Sarah smiled as best she could and nodded. Her father, next to her, nodded to the Sheriff in thanks.

"So," he said, turning to the crowd, "any questions?"

LATER THAT NIGHT, as Sarah Charles lay in her bed, she clutched her teddy bear tightly to her chest. The same blue, threadbare teddy she discarded in the back of her cupboard many years previous. Before, it symbolized her childhood. Being fifteen, she had embraced womanhood with poise, but tonight, and ever since the events in Cromwell Woods—the Dead Woods as everyone at school called them—she had needed the comfort of her youth back.

With her head on her pillow, she gazed at the curtained window on the far side of her bedroom. The night outside now felt terrifying to her. Only a day ago, she had loved the darkness. Loved the town at night. Felt safe everywhere. But everything had changed. For the first time, she slept with her window locked tightly and the curtains closed, something she never did before. Even on the coldest night, she needed the window open, the breeze drifting in. Now, she shut the dark out, shut the shadows out, and blocked any sight of the enormous monster lying in wait outside. That monster that was, in fact, a large oak tree. One that spread its branches out past her bedroom window. Branches she was now terrified of. Terrified that she would see the furious and awful face of the Tree Man. The thing they had once joked about so freely.

As her eyes closed, her thoughts drifted to Mikey. Now her friend lay in an induced coma in the hospital. His legs had been amputated, as all the flesh on them had been eaten clean off the bone when he was found lying unconscious in the clearing. Sarah hoped he slept through all of it, and when he would eventually wake, she prayed his memory would be blank of what he went through.

Matt had been kept at home by his parents, retreating into himself and keeping silent since their return from the station. They did not want Sarah visiting him, nor anyone. They wanted to protect him.

As for Gerry, she could not bring herself to imagine anything. The last she saw of him, he was staring at them from the tree line, vines spewing out of his mouth like giant, thorny tentacles--a terrible sight she couldn't shake from her mind, despite attempts by authority figures to convince her she'd imagined it.

"The mental stress of the situation has created this fantasy of ghosts and monsters," the police-assigned therapist had informed her father. "It did that to protect her. It's quite natural. She'll remember more clearly over time."

But Sarah knew this was not caused by stress. It was not make-believe. What she saw was *real*. The Tree Man was *real*. What happened to Gerry was *real*. The danger in the dead woods was *real*. How could it be a bear, coyote, or whatever the townsfolk presumed it to be? She had no answers to the logical questions. She did not have answers to anything anymore.

THE GROTESQUERY

In the clubhouse, Emmie, James, Hamish, and Findley sat in a circle upon the worn shag-pile rug. A space had been left between Emmie and Hamish—a space reserved for Pip. None of them wanted to believe their friend would not be coming back. They each wished for everything to revert to how it had been a week before.

Emmie held Pip's journal in her lap, open to the last entry. She read from the pages aloud as everyone listened intently.

"I can't believe I've delivered the paper to Mrs. Petrie for so long. I haven't once spoken to her about anything except getting paid. She must be so lonely in her house," Emmie paused, as she began to feel a swell of emotion. Pushing her upset down, she swallowed, then continued. "She must be all alone in her house, with reminders of Adam and his dad everywhere. She must be so sad. I'm gonna go and speak to her tomorrow. I remember one of Dad's sermons. One of the few I actually believe in. He said something like, 'Hell is loneliness; Heaven is knowing someone is there.' I think I agree with that. I wish I'd known Adam better before he died. It feels like such a waste, him dying. He just went, just like that. Gone. He left a hole where he used to be. But only for his mom." Emmie looked up at her friends. "And that's it. Last entry."

"That seals it, right?" Findley asked. "We know he went there. Pip says it there in black and white."

"No one said he didn't," James chipped in. "We *know* he went there."

"But we didn't know it was to do with Adam," Findley posited. "What if she went mad when he mentioned her kid, and then... You know."

Emmie flicked back a page in the journal and scanned the handwriting, using her finger as a guide.

"What about Pip's mom?" Hamish asked as he looked at Findley. "What about those dead wood things she spoke about?"

"I dunno what to think about any of this," James said. "It's insane."

"Here's something else," Emmie said as she read a passage from the journal. "My mom's definitely *not* lying about Adam. I remember what she said about it like it was yesterday. I even remember her arguing with the Sheriff about it. But *he said* she was wrong despite seeing those bite marks as well."

Findley shook his head. "I've no idea what we should do, but I think we gotta go see his mom."

"We gotta find out what the dead wood stuff's about," Emmie added. "What if Pip's mom's right?"

"And what are you gonna say to her when we march up there?" James asked. "Hey, Mrs. Petrie, can you please tell us what happened to Pip? You smiled at me at the station, so I know you're lying. Now fess up, or... Or what? Oh, and Pip's mom thinks there are some monsters in the woods, you know about 'em too?" He shook his head. "It makes us sound like we need to be locked away."

Findley went to answer but then shrugged in frustration. "I have no shuckin' idea what the hell we need to do," he said, using his invented profanity. "None of it makes any sense. Pip's mom sounded so scared. So... Believable."

"There's only one thing we *can* do here," Emmie said as she closed the journal and put it on the rug in front of her crossed legs. "We gotta do what we did at Pip's. We look for clues."

"Are you kiddin'?" Hamish said, stunned. "Break in? You're kiddin'. You *gotta* be kiddin'."

Emmie shrugged her shoulders as a weak smile crept upon her face. "Maybe we have to do it? But if we *do*, we should wait until his mom goes out, not just go in like we did at Pips."

"And what are we looking for exactly? A body?" James asked. But as he did, everyone fell silent, realizing it could indeed happen in a world of infinite possibilities.

"We can't all go around breaking into people's houses," Hamish added. "We can't do that. It's not right. Besides, after what you heard from Pip's mom. You think I'm going *near* that place? Didn't she say whatever it was in the woods reached out to Adam's house?"

"Hamish, it'll be okay," James reassured him.

"If any of you think I'm going near there, you're all mad. No way." Hamish stood his ground, feeling the fear intensely. "It's how horror movies start; the stupid people don't listen to the damn obvious warnings."

"C'mon, we've been there lots of times," Emmie said. "There's nothing wrong with the woods. Hell, we were there last week!"

"So, Pip's mom's what? Lying?" Hamish was getting more angry than shocked that none of his friends also saw this as a stupid move. "Then why were you freaked out after hearing what she said? You believed it too."

"We're not saying she's lying," Findley explained. "She really thinks there're ghosts or whatever there. Zombie dogs. It's not a lie, cos she honestly believes what she says. She's just wrong. So, why was I freaked out?" He nodded in Emmie's direction. "Cos it was heckin' scary. That's why. Last Halloween, when we had a sleepover at Emmie's? Remember we watched the clown thing on TV? You got scared bad at that, right?"

"And?" Hamish replied.

"And, you were scared when you were *there*," Findley's voice fell to a whisper. "But do you believe it's real, actually *real*? The clown, you think he's coming after you? You think he *actually* turned into a big spider? Now you are no longer in front of that TV? You still believe it? Cos you believed it then!"

Hamish didn't answer.

"So, yeah, we were freaked out. Freaked far out... But you wanna know what was scarier than all the ghost stuff? What really got to me?"

Hamish maintained his silence.

"Despite all the haunted tree talk. Despite everything she said, truth or not, it means I'm not imagining what I saw at the police station. It means Pip's mom also believes Adam's mom knows what happened. She *knows* about what happened to Pip. And the part that's really getting to me? *If* Adam's mom does know? If she knows about Pip? Then the chances are almost *certain* Pip is... That he's—" Findley could not finish his sentence. He did not have to. It was apparent what he meant to say.

"You know... We don't *have* to go to her house or the woods," James chimed in as he looked sheepishly around at his friends, hesitant about putting this particular thought across. "Remember those other names Pip's mom mentioned? Can't we just ask *them* about the woods instead? What did that poster above Ms. Abara's desk say? Assumption is the mother of all mistakes? Why don't we see if it's just Pip's mom or if anyone else thinks the same as her."

"You got a point." Emmie nodded.

"Are you winning this argument based on our math teacher's poster?" Findley couldn't help but be amused. "I guess I can't argue." Turning to Hamish, he said: "You good? No woods yet? Just plain ol' detective work?"

"Much better plan," Hamish said. "But who was it we gotta talk to? Who did she say?"

"It was a bit tough to make out," Emmie replied. "But I think it was Gerry someone-or-other and Mike Fish? We probably better go to the library and check some records or something. If one of Pip's mom's friends *did* die, there'd be a trace of it. Some report. Some paper talkin' about it."

"I hate to say it... But the guy's surname... Mike... It's Fisk, not Fish," James added with a sigh. "Mikey Fisk. You know him. We all do."

Hamish, Emmie, and Findley stared back at James. Each of them very confused.

"I'll give you a clue," James said, trying to hide his trepidation. "He's the one guy we're *not* allowed to visit."

Their confusion fell to a horrid realization.

"Oh no," Hamish muttered. "No, no, no. Not *him*. Not Mad Mike."

THE FOLLOWING DAY, the winter sun reared into the icy sky again, overstaying its welcome into the spring months, bringing brightness but no warmth. The sunny yet freezing weather held the town of Hemlock Creek hostage in its unseasonable grip and forced everyone to wear their winter clothing for weeks after they normally would. It was as if the daylight had been trapped behind thick glass, forced only to be seen over the town, unable to do anything except witness the townsfolk go about their business.

For Findley, the walk across town filled him with dread. He felt like a death row prisoner walking to his execution. His legs felt more like Jell-O with each step he took. He felt weaker and weaker the closer to Lamplight Crescent he and his friends got. But he was not alone. They all felt reluctant to be here. At this moment, Findley would have preferred risking getting arrested for breaking and entering Mrs. Petrie's house.

MICHAEL JASON FISK. Mikey Fisk. Known colloquially to the town of Hemlock Creek as 'Mad Mike,' he was someone people were actively told to avoid. Not that they had to try hard—most people had never *actually* seen Mad Mike. They knew *of* him and learned to avoid the dilapidated house at the end of Lamplight Crescent at all costs. Everyone had been told by their parents to steer clear, even the police said the same. They didn't even say the same about the dam or the quarry, all places that were infinitely more dangerous.

The tales from the people who *had* met him fueled the town's rumor mill; Albert, the grocery store delivery boy, who dropped off regular food parcels. Sandy Channing, the latest in an long line of welfare volunteers, who had to visit Mike once a week to not only check on him, but also clean as much of his mess as they could brave. Each person told similar stories. Each described the same scene: a barely dressed, unkempt man, covered in sores and dirt, slumped on a moldy old sofa chair. His leg stumps were covered in leaking pustules and scabs. On one side of his chair sat a pile of used plastic urine bottles. Some had fallen over, and some overflowed onto the threadbare carpet. Each contained a dark yellow liquid that filled the room with a thick, ammonia-like stench; in the trash can on the other side of the chair, rotten food mixed with the brown lumps of Mad Mike's waste, without any care for health or cleanliness. The welfare volunteers could only replace the bottles with fresh ones and empty the bins. Anything else they tried to do was an exercise in futility. The house itself was in too grotesque a state for any cleaning to make any real difference. The dirt and grime from years of neglect were so ingrained the whole building would have to be razed to the ground and rebuilt from scratch to cleanse the area well enough. Everyone deemed Mad Mike's house a diseased pit where no one should risk their health going. Not to mention that Mad Mike lived up to his name with aplomb. He had left his sanity, along with his legs, on that fateful day back in 1968.

Anyone who went to Mad Mike's house spoke of an encroaching dread as they stood on the porch. Before the man's stench could even hit them, everyone somehow subconsciously knew, deep in their bones, they should not be there. They should run. As fast as they could in the opposite direction and never return.

THE DOOR in front of them lay open. The fall leaves from the surrounding trees had been blowing in from the outside for some time, filling the hallway. The house was permanently open to the elements.

"I wanna go home," Hamish whispered. No one disagreed or argued, as they all felt an identical sense of dread standing at the doorway to Mad Mike's rotting abode.

However, Emmie was not looking inside the open front door like the others. Her gaze fell instead to the left of the house, to the line of thick woods beyond the backyards of all the homes on this side of the street. The line of dense, *dead* woods. "Any of you know the woods were right there? Right next to this house?"

Their attention was pulled away from the house in front of them, to where Emmie stare aimed. Her eyes were glassy and wide as her anxiety built up within, and theirs soon followed suit, as they saw the trees.

"Oh God," James whimpered.

"It's all make-believe," Findley said, attempting to soothe his own fears. "Just trees out there. No monsters."

"Let's get this over with," James said as he showed some uncharacteristic chutzpah by taking a few steps forward. "Mr. Fisk?" he called out into the house.

The other three were shocked back to reality as a weak voice slithered out of the house toward them.

"Hello?" the strangled and broken voice said. Without waiting for a reply, it repeated. "*Hello?*"

James' nerve suddenly fell away as he turned to Emmie, unable to answer.

"Mr. Fisk," Findley called out, taking over. "Can we ask you a couple of questions, please?"

There was no response from inside.

Findley glanced at his friends. "We didn't plan this well, at all," he whispered.

"We want to ask you about the dead woods?" Emmie called out as she grimaced, expecting the man inside to shout at them.

Again, no response.

"And about Gerry?" Findley added. Then, like Emmie, he immediately braced for an angry retort.

"Just give me a moment," the voice inside the house said chirpily, without a trace of anger or contempt. "I have to make myself presentable."

Unable to bring themselves to answer him, the four of them turned to look at each other.

"Everyone... Stay close," Emmie whispered. "First sign of *anything*, we turn and run."

Hamish's hands trembled. "This was a bad, bad idea."

"We could run now, right? Just get out of here?" Findley half-joked, but inside meant every single word. Hamish wanted to agree with his friends suggestion, but had no time to speak up.

"For Pip," James said. "We *gotta* do this for Pip."

"Screw it," Emmie nodded. "It's only a man, right? What's the worst that's gonna happen?"

But no one knew. None of them had ever seen Mad Mike. They had only heard the stories. The images in each of their heads were undoubtedly a thousand times worse than what the reality *actually* was. That is what Emmie tried to convince herself of.

"Come in," the slimy voice called from deep inside the decaying old house.

.   .   .

As THEY STEPPED down the muddy hallway of the house on Lamplight Crescent, Findley, James, Emmie, and Hamish all stuck together as tightly as they could.

The reek of sweat, rot, and waste hit them almost instantly. The warm funk of putrefaction invaded their nostrils and got more potent with each passing moment.

"You have to forgive me," the gnarled voice seeped out of the doorway ahead of them, wafting out on the miasma of horrible odors. "I'm fatigued... Please, come inside."

As the group approached the doorless frame of the room where the voice came from, they were finally met with the sight of 'Mad' Mike Fisk.

Only wearing a pair of black, damp, oversized shorts, his exposed and distended belly hung forward over the threadbare cotton waistline. Bloated so solidly, his stomach looked as if it was ready to burst. His bare arms looked as if they once held some muscle definition, but were now almost skeletal, with graying and blotchy skin loosely covering his frame.

His legs had been removed at differing lengths, one right above the knee, the other halfway up his femur. Where the wounds should have healed over, having been operated on decades previously, his legs were instead coated in open lesions and boils, with blackened skin trailing up into his shorts.

This man's face was no less grotesque. With most of his teeth missing, his face hung down from his skull, looking as ill-fitting as his shorts. A long black and gray beard grew out of his recessed chin, as wild as the woodland outside, growing like an immense cobweb. The thickness of his beard contrasted the small wispy collection of hair that flailed on top of his liver-spotted bald pate. All this grotesquery was topped off with his nose, or lack thereof. Having collapsed in on itself long ago, the hole where his nose once sat gave him a genuinely skeletal and otherworldly appearance. In all, he was now a terrifying echo of the boy he once was—the boy who ventured into the woods with Sarah, Gerry, and Matt decades before.

Around the stained and worn seat, beyond the urine jars and bin of waste, the room itself was as open to the elements as the hallway. The walls around him had given in to nature, and vines had broken their way in from the outside. Thick branches had forced themselves through the plaster at multiple points and spread their way into the very fabric of the house. The cracks the plants grew through were broad and could easily fit a hand through them, far enough to touch the outside air.

Curiously—as Emmie noticed—beyond this horrifying man now sat staring expectantly at them was the lack of any other objects in the room. There was no television. There were no books or magazines. There were no pictures on the walls. No shelves. No tables. Nothing. It was only this man, his seat, and the waste receptacles.

"Who are you?" The man said, his bloodshot eyes fixed on each of them in turn. "And why do you want to know about my good friend, Gerry?"

The four all stood facing 'Mad' Mike Fisk, each feeling extreme discomfort at where they were, what they could see, and what they were forced to smell.

"I—" Findley said first, trying not to show his disgust. "My name's Findley Scott."

Mad Mike smiled a gap-toothed smile. "Findley? From the Old Gaelic *Fionn* and *Lagh*: meaning beautiful hero? Yes?"

Findley only stared, not knowing how to react.

"We can all see you are indeed beautiful," Mad Mike said with lustful glee. "But tell me, boy, are you a hero?"

"I–" was all Findley could utter before Emmaleen interrupted.

"My name is Emmie, Emmaleen. It means peaceful home," she said, almost tripping over her words. "We're here as we want—"

"I want *never* gets, young lady," Mad Mike cut in with a smile that turned so thin-lipped it looked almost cruel. His voice boomed in anger. "I invited you into my home, and you talk out of turn? Did pigs raise you? How *dare* you!"

Emmie's stomach dropped as she froze, not knowing what to say.

James's mouth dropped open, shocked and offended. He nudged Findley and spoke, not caring if Mad Mike might hear him. "Let's go. This is stupid. We don't need him."

Mike's cruel smile suddenly fell as his bravado dropped. "No, please!" he yelled out. "I'm only joking. All is good between us, friends." He nodded to Emmie, his smile almost panicking. "All is happy, yes? Emmaleen, you say? Great friends."

Findley stepped forward and spoke, "Look, we just want to ask—"

"Who are the other two?" Mike leaned forward and stared at them in turn. "We have Findley and Emmaleen, and?"

James tutted, "I'm James," he motioned to Hamish with a nod, "and this is Hamish. We wanna ask you about the Cromwell Woods. We think our friend may be mixed up in the same thing. I—" James' words trailed off as he noticed

Mike staring at Hamish, instead of listening to anything he said. Mike's drool-covered lips mouthed the word 'Hamish' over and over.

Hamish, meanwhile, was terrified at this sudden attention. He wanted to run and scream but could only stand in fear, being ogled at.

Findley and Emmie both glanced at each other.

"Hamish is Scottish," Mike said, still staring. "Do you know what it means?" He continued without waiting for a reply. "I am a believer in fate... And I... I did not notice until you said his name... I believe Hamish was always meant to come here. I didn't think it could be true. But here you are."

"Can you tell us about the woods or not?" James asked.

With a flash of annoyance, Mike's eyes darted to him. "Hamish may ask what he wishes. You can keep *quiet*."

"Fine," James said.

"Go on," Emmie whispered to Hamish as she nudged his arm. "Ask him."

"Yes, Hamish, ask me," Mike said, gleefully resuming his stare. "You are not scared of me, are you?"

In the few moments of silence that followed, Mad Mike did not blink, move, or alter his glare.

After swallowing what felt to him like a mountain of dry sand, Hamish eventually managed to find his voice. "I-I," he said. "I mean, *we* wanted to know—"

"Yes?" Mike leaned more forward in his rotten chair. "What did you want to know?"

"The dead woods, I mean Cromwell Woods."

"*Yes?*" Mike's smile grew wider as a string of thick yellow drool passed over his lips and dribbled into his unruly beard.

"We heard something, like a ghost or something, took

your friend?" Hamish tried to ignore the cold shiver running down his spine, but his voice stuttered as he spoke. "And. A-and your... L-legs."

"You heard that?" Mike asked, not showing any reaction. "Ghosts took my legs?"

"Our f-friend has gone missing," Hamish continued.

"You see—" was all Findley could cut in with before Mad Mike raised his broken nailed finger and held it up to silence Findley.

Mike then moved his finger to point at Hamish without saying a word and gave him a cue to continue with one motion. It was apparent Mad Mike would not listen to anybody else.

Hamish turned to his friends. Emmie motioned with a smile for him to carry on. Having no choice but to turn back to the disgusting man, Hamish took a steadying breath. "Our friend disappeared where A-Adam Petrie died... And the w-woods—"

Raising his hand, Mad Mike shook his head dismissively. "I haven't heard this nonsense for a long time, but it is still that... *Nonsense.*" He rolled his eyes with a shake of his head. "People say there are monsters in the trees, that the dead roam the woods waiting to kill trespassers. Well, I know better than anyone *what* is in there," he motioned to his legs or lack thereof. "Nothing. Nothing except old rotten wood. That's it. Whatever the animal attacked me has long gone. You can go in there whenever you want. You could even go now. In fact, why don't you go there now?"

"An animal?" Findley asked, taken aback by this revelation.

"You think anything else did this?" Mike asked,

rhetorically. "And from what you say, that young boy Adam, too?"

"His dog killed him," Emmie corrected.

"His dead dog?" James added.

Mad Mike sighed. "You would easily believe something undead killed your friend, rather than a murderer or a wild animal? Can you hear how stupid you sound?"

The four did not answer.

"Now I know we all have our own wild beliefs, I'm sure," Mad Mike began, almost lecturing. "Some believe in a God, some believe in aliens, some in tree beasts. Even I have such a belief."

No one replied.

"Do you want to know what it is I believe?" Mike asked.

Silence.

Mike frowned. "Someone should ask me what it is."

Nothing.

"Someone *better* ask me what it is." His demeanor and change of tone became intimidating.

"What d'you believe?" James asked without even thinking, merely reacting to the situation.

"Oh, I am happy to answer," Mike replied. His intimidating tone immediately flipping back to happy. "I *believe* in nature. I *believe* in everything being linked by the very fabric of creation. There are no ghosts, there are no evil bushes, nothing. There is nature and, in this case, occasional poor, hungry animals." He took a breath and shifted in his chair. "If someone dies around nature, then it is not through malice, but happenstance. Myself, I was a victim of a natural animal. Not a haunted bit of woodland. Gerry, my dear friend. He suffered the same fate as me, but he lost his life. And the boy you mentioned... *A ghost dog*?

That's not only ignorant to believe but very foolish and dangerous to think. You need to each look at yourselves long and hard in the mirror and realize how impossible your flights of fancy are. You are all being naïve. Ghosts? Monsters? Bah!"

The four began to realize the same thing at once silently. Even though he was disgusting, he spoke more sensibly than they expected.

"Hamish, dear boy, could you do me a favor?" Mike asked, his sickly smile now showing all of the few teeth in his mouth. "Stay behind for a moment while the others leave."

"Hell no," Findley blurted.

Mike turned to face him with an unimpressed expression. "I have a piece of information that may help you all in your quest... However misguided. But I do not like you. Or *her*." He pointed at Emmie, then to James. "Or that other rude one there. But Hamish, I will trust."

They all glanced at Hamish, who looked more scared by the second.

Mike continued. "He will be right behind you. I only need him for thirty seconds, one-minute tops."

Though terrified, though barely able to speak without a stutter, Hamish turned to his friends. "It's o-okay," he mumbled. "F-for Pip."

SPLINTER & VINE

When Hamish appeared out from the filth of Mad Mike Fisk's house, Emmie nearly rushed over and threw her arms around him. Findley and James, too, felt the same wave of relief wash over them as they saw their friend step off the rotten porch and onto the overgrown lawn, where they all waited.

"We nearly called the cops," James said. "You okay? He didn't try anything, did he?"

Hamish smiled weakly. "I'm okay. He's just lonely."

"What?" Findley exclaimed. "He's a mad old coot rotting away in his own stink in a gross old house."

Hamish shrugged. "Not arguing with that."

"As long as you're okay," Emmie said as she went to put her arm over his shoulder. But when she did, he recoiled from her. "What the hell?" she said. "What I do?"

Not having seen this reaction, James motioned to the house. "So, what he say? What's so important he'd only talk to you?"

"Nothing much," Hamish replied. "Said we needed to go back to the woods. The trees... They're lonely or something. Then he talked about how flowers get sad when left alone."

"What?" Findley said deadpan. "Sad? Are you kidding me?"

"It's strange," Hamish replied. "When he was talkin', it kinda all made sense. Now I'm here; it's all just..."

"Stupid?" James said.

Overlooking Hamish's recoiling from her, Emmie's

attention turned to something on his neck. She pointed at it. "Wait, what's that on your neck?" Leaning in, she squinted as she tried to focus on the mark. "That a splinter?"

"What?" Hamish replied, moving his fingers to his neck.

James and Findley peered over and saw it too.

"Where the hell d'ya get a splinter in your neck from?" James asked.

"Dunno," Hamish replied, sounding gradually more panicked. As his fingers touched the mark, he winced as the pain hit. "Ow! Goddamn it!"

Findley turned to Hamish, then to the house. "What did he do to you, Hamish?" he asked.

"I told you, he didn't do squat!" Hamish, still wincing, answered with a note of annoyance.

"Maybe you got it in the clubhouse?" James asked.

"Let's get home; we can talk about this when we're not a few feet away from that stink, okay?" Emmie said, then turned to Hamish. "Your folks are home, right?"

Hamish nodded.

Without another word, they all turned to walk away from Mad Mike's house. But as they did, a police car pulled up on the curb at the end of the drive in front of them.

"You *did* call the cops!" Hamish exclaimed in shock, cradling his neck with his hand and cupping it over the splinter.

"Wasn't us," James said.

Out of the driver's side of the patrol car, Sheriff Benson appeared, wearing shades and sheriff's hat. He closed the car door behind him as he shook his head, looking at them all standing on the lawn.

"Damn it," he grimaced to himself. He then called out to them. "Get over here!"

With their heads hung downward, and with slow movement, the four walked toward the Sheriff, knowing they had been caught in a no-go zone. As they stepped off the unkempt lawn and onto the sidewalk, he addressed them sternly, clearly annoyed. "What the hell are you doing here? I thought I made it clear to *everyone* that *no one* comes here. It's for your own safety, you understand?"

"We know," Emmie said, not meeting the Sheriff's gaze.

"It's not healthy in there," Matt said as he looked up at the house, then back down at them. "I'm glad I caught you before you went in."

After a few seconds of silence, the truth dawned on Matt. Looking at their expressions, he then could see he was too late. Their guilt was glaringly obvious.

"Really? You went in?" the Sheriff sighed loudly.

They didn't reply.

"Well, what happened?" Matt continued. "And you better be truthful, cos I had to hear about this from a neighbor, and I don't want it to become something it doesn't need to be, you get me? I don't wanna drag you all in for trespassing or nothin'."

James peered up at the house on the other side of the street. He noticed a curtain twitch as someone hid from sight as they saw him clock their spying.

Findley was the first to reply. "We went cos of Pip."

"As *you're* involved, Findley, I figured as much," Matt said as he shook his head in exasperation. "I guess I should be glad you're just here and not harassing poor Mrs. Petrie."

James shuffled uncomfortably.

"Now, why here?" Matt asked. "What the hell does that man have to do with anything?"

Findley glanced at Emmie.

"Don't look at *her*," Matt said as he approached them. "You're talking to me, okay?"

"We heard—" Findley couldn't finish his sentence. He knew it would just mean more trouble.

"Pip used to say that Mike Fisk knew about the woods. Said his mom said so," Emmie said. Her lies were convincing even to her. "And he disappeared near the woods, so we thought, why not ask him? We had to. We know Pip didn't run away. He—"

"Okay, okay," Matt said as he exhaled loudly. He then noticed Hamish holding his neck. "What's up with you?" he asked.

Hamish half-smiled as the pain in his neck started to throb.

"He got a splinter," James said.

Matt removed his sunglasses and bent down to Hamish, "Let's see it," he commanded.

Hamish removed his hand from his neck with care, and the Sheriff took a closer look at the mark.

"Yup," Matt said as he squinted at the wound. "That's a doozy. In quite deep by the looks of it. Must hurt like hell,"

Hamish nodded.

"Well, get in the car. I'll drive you all back home, okay?" the Sheriff said, putting a hand on Hamish's shoulder. "Your folks may need to take you to Urgent Care if they can't get it out, but you'll probably be fine with just a pair of tweezers."

. . .

HAVING DROPPED everyone at their respective houses, Sheriff Benson turned his car around and drove to Lamplight Crescent, back to Mad Mike Fisk's house.

With the sun now setting, he grimaced as he shut off his engine and looked up at the dilapidated house. Without light or a sign of life, the place looked as derelict as the man who sat inside.

It took all of the Sheriff's nerve to walk up to the porch, let alone call out into the open hallway.

"Mikey, it's Matt," he shouted into the darkened house. "I'm coming in."

Without waiting for a reply, he instinctively put his hand on the butt of his holstered pistol, then cautiously stepped over the threshold to the house and onto the dirt and leaf-covered hallway.

"I know I don't have to tell you," Matt spoke again, taking each step into the dark house with careful hesitance. "You know I'm a cop, and I have a gun. So don't try anything."

As the light faded and it got harder to see, Matt pulled a pencil-sized flashlight from his belt and switched it on. Its weak beam broke through the darkness with only minimal effect, enough for him to see where he was going.

"You gonna say anything?" he called out again.

No reply.

SITTING AT THE KITCHEN COUNTER, Hamish looked miserable as his fathers fussed over him. Kristofer was busily pouring a measure of boiling water into a bowl while Simon, wearing his reading glasses, stared at the mark on his son's neck.

"What in the world do you kids get up to?" Simon said, sounding almost impressed at Hamish's injury. "When I was young, the most I got was a scraped knee."

"You were never young," Kristofer joked, placing a bowl on the counter with a cloth.

Smirking at the joke, Simon dipped the cloth in hot water for a few seconds. He looked kindly at Hamish. "Now, this will be hot," he said. "But we have to moisten your skin up, okay? It'll make it easier to pull the splinter out."

Hamish merely nodded. The pain had gone from throbbing to booming throughout his body. It pulsed out from where the splinter lay and worsened with every beat of his heart.

"Poor baby," Kristofer said as he kissed Hamish's head.

"You got the tweezers?" Simon asked, keeping his emotions at bay to ensure Hamish remained calm.

DOWN THE HALLWAY, Sheriff Benson stepped cautiously nearer to the open living room door. In the dark, with his flashlight showing the dirt and decay in its illuminated focus, the whole building seemed like a film set for a haunted house. Almost too stereotypical to be realistic in how horrible it was.

"Mikey, answer me... You think you're being funny, but you're not!" the Sheriff said, almost sounding scared. The smell from within the house hit him hard as he got nearer to the living room. The stench of bodily waste and rot smothered him, making it hard for him not to wretch.

·   ·   ·

As Simon held the tweezers, Kristofer shined a torch at Hamish's embedded splinter. With a cold sweat breaking out on his forehead, Simon moved the metal instrument closer and closer, concentrating.

"You okay, baby?" Kristofer asked, worried.

"It hurts," Hamish said, whimpering.

Simon gritted his teeth as he fought to keep his focus. He pushed down his worry as far down as it could go.

"It'll be all okay soon enough," Kristofer reassured with a tremble.

Entering the living room, the Sheriff shone his torch around. He coughed as the smell hit the back of his throat. It had been a few years since he last had cause to walk in this house, and he now prayed to any God who may listen that he would never have to come back here again.

"Where are you?" Matt asked under his breath as he shone the light across the room, scanning it slowly. The branches that broke through the walls cast shadows that looked almost like immense spider legs. Matt intently ignored this but felt an extreme sense of unease.

Suddenly the beam shone directly over Mad Mike Fisk, sitting in his chair, causing Matt to reel backward in shock. The hue from the flashlight made this legless and dirty man appear almost demonic with all the haunting shadows cast around him.

"Goddamn it!" the Sheriff exclaimed. "You think it's funny, Mikey?

"Oh, Matthew," Mad Mike said, sounding on the verge of sleep. "Why did it take you so long to come and see me? Do you not like me anymore?"

. . .

Simon stared at Hamish with his mouth agape.

Kristofer looked confused.

"What did you say, son?" Simon asked, unable to hide the worry in his voice.

Hamish stared forward blankly. "You don't need to be afraid, Matthew. They won't hurt you as long as I am here."

Simon shot a glance at Kristofer, who was almost in tears.

"Just get it out!" Kristofer shouted with worry.

"What did you say to those kids, Mikey?" the Sheriff asked, keeping his hand on the butt of his holstered pistol.

"Are you afraid, Matthew?" Mad Mike's voice, though weak, sounded decidedly perverse with glee. "What do you think I could do to you? What would you like me to do to you? Do you think I would let them take you?"

"He must be having fever dreams or something," Simon said in a panic.

"*Simon, get it out, please!*" Kristofer pleaded.

"I'm trying," Simon barked back as he moved the tweezers in for a second attempt. "It's stuck right in there!"

"I told them nothing about the Tree Man if that's what you want to know?" Hamish said. His voice sounded as horribly gleeful as Mad Mike's.

"Well, what *did* you tell them?" The Sheriff asked.

. . .

"I TOLD them it was a wild animal," Hamish replied. "Exactly as you asked me to. To forget the truth and tell a lie. For the greater good, yes?"

"Got it!" Simon said as the tweezers grabbed one end of the splinter in his son's neck.

"What else do you want, Matthew?" Hamish said, his voice sounding like he was about to laugh.

"YOU KNOW WHAT," the Sheriff replied. "I let you stay here in this filth under one condition and one condition alone."

"I KNOW what you choose to tell yourself, Matthew," Hamish replied. "But we both know it is because you fear what I would do. What I would let them do."

At that instant, Simon squeezed on the tweezers and pulled the splinter from Hamish's neck. But as it came out of the flesh, both of Hamish's fathers looked stunned at how long the object was. It was nearly 3 inches in length and embedded deep in their son's neck.

Kristofer gasped in horror.

"THIS PLACE IS A DEATH TRAP," Matt said as the smell grew more horrific. "One of them got a splinter from here. It better not be your doing. I have no idea what you are up to. But I don't trust you."

. . .

"OH MATTHEW, YOU ARE SO HURTFUL," Hamish continued as he began to laugh a sickly laugh. "I like *you*."

MAD MIKE LAUGHED the same laugh from his rotten chair.

"What's so funny?" the Sheriff demanded.

After getting louder and louder, creepier and creepier, the laugh suddenly ceased. Stopped dead in its tracks. Unnaturally so. Mike's smile fell away to reveal a scared frown.

Then, Mike spoke. Unlike before, his voice was suddenly weak and terrified, barely sounding like himself. "Daddies?" he said in a child-like whimper. "What's happening to me?" As he finished his sentence, Mike lost consciousness and slumped in his seat as if a switch inside him had been turned off.

"BABY!" Kristofer cried out and held onto Hamish, slumped unconscious onto the kitchen chair. His complexion was pallid, and his breathing was getting gradually shallower.

"I'll get the car," Simon said as he scrambled to his feet.

"Hurry!" Kristofer cried out as he cradled his son.

His tear-filled gaze then turned to the countertop at the long dark splinter on its tiled surface.

IT WAS ten o'clock in the evening, and Emmie was sitting on the floor in Findley's bedroom. He stood by the window, looking out in the direction of James' house.

"They should have let him stay over," Findley murmured in annoyance. Turning to Emmie, he shook his head. "Makes no sense. Why keep him in his room alone?"

"They want to protect him," Emmie shrugged. "I get it."

"Keep him in jail, ya mean?" He walked over and sat on the edge of the bed, facing her. "They think Pip ran, they think he will too?"

"I'm sure the Sheriff told 'em about Mad Mike," Emmie countered as she stared at her shoes. "They're probably just keeping him away from that place, or from us, or something."

"I guess," Findley said. "Only wish he was here."

After a long pause, Findley moved off the bed and sat on the floor closer to Emmie. "Let's work it out," he began. "Cops say Pip ran away; we know that."

"Yeah," Emmie replied.

"But it can't be the case 'cos of his journal, right? That's what we said?"

Emmie nodded.

"If I'm being honest, I think it's a crappy theory. So what? He left a book. Would he care about it if he was messed up enough to run away? It's not strong evidence."

"Oh, thank God," Emmie said, relieved. "I thought I was the only one thinking it. I just went along cos everyone else did."

"It was the old stinky guy that changed my mind," he said as he smiled. "Gross ol' shucker spoke some sense about us needing to be rational about this."

"Yeah," Emmie looked concerned. "But it's not like Pip to run. Or take money. Is it?"

"Oh, I still think he didn't run. I just think our evidence needs to be a bit better and not about dead dogs and ghosts," Findley said, lowering his voice. "Adam's mom has to know what happened, or at least know more than she let on."

"And what about Pip's mom? All the stuff she said?"

"If a mad old coot sitting in his own pee don't believe it, then..." Findley then thought for a second and chuckled. "And speaking of that... That stink. What the hell was it?"

"I think we all know what it was, Fin," Emmie said, unable to contain her laughter.

"Is that what the trash can was for?"

Their fun was halted as the bedroom door opened. Without turning, Findley said, "We'll go to bed in a sec, okay?"

His mother, Amber, stood in the open doorway. She looked distraught, but holding it together as best she could. "Fin?" she said. "Emmie?"

Turning his head to her, Fin felt his stomach drop. He knew that expression. He had seen it before. Something terrible had happened.

"You both should come downstairs, okay?" she said. "It's about Hamish."

St. Bernard's Hospital stood on the outskirts of Hemlock Creek. Being a small medical facility in a small town, its staff were few, yet high in passion for their work, even if their careers had never progressed them beyond the confines of the county.

The whole building would have been almost silent on a typical night this close to midnight. The patients asleep and visiting hours long since passed. Tonight, the sound of crying and wailing echoed through the halls—all coming from the waiting room of the emergency room. Sleeping patients had woken up to these distraught cries. Still, instead of complaining, they lay in their beds in silence, allowing those making the sounds to accept their grief. To accept what cruel hand nature had dealt them.

It was not death that caused these cries, though, for Hamish was still in the land of the living. He was instead asleep. A deep comatic sleep from which he would not wake any time soon.

Kristofer Flynn cried loudly in the ER waiting room as he clung to his husband. Hugging him tightly and without any plan of letting him go.

"My sweet baby," he cried into Simon's shoulder.

On the seats opposite them, Findley and Emmie held hands next to his mother, Amber. All three looked upset, but they also had no idea what they could do to help or what good their presence did for Hamish or his parents. But they were there anyway. They felt they had to be. And they did not want to leave. They were the only people in the waiting room.

"James should be here," Findley said morosely under his breath.

Hearing him, his mother whispered, "I'll talk to his parents tomorrow, okay? It's a bit late to wake them up now."

Still hugging his husband, Simon looked at Amber kindly as Kristofer wept. "Thank you for coming, Amber, and bringing the kids. I know Hamish would be thrilled to know you're all here."

Amber smiled and nodded.

A doctor walked out the double doors to the waiting room and over to them. A stout woman in her sixties, she looked exhausted.

"Mr. Flynn?" the doctor said.

Looking up from his crying, Kristofer turned to look up at the doctor, as did everyone else.

"Your son is comfortable, and we're running all the tests we can to find out what's wrong," she said. "But we still have to wait and see, I'm afraid. I know how hard it is for you—for all of you—but we must play it safe until we know what happened and how we can fix it."

"Play it safe?" Kristofer sniffed as he spoke. "Safe how?"

"Well," the doctor shrugged. "We have given Hamish some full-spectrum antibiotics to fight any infection. We've also scheduled an x-ray—"

"What? Why?" Simon interrupted.

"To see if there are any more foreign bodies in him," she explained. "You said he did not know where he got the splinter, so he could have more; we don't know. And more could be the reason behind his current condition. We don't expect to find anything, but we must ensure nothing is missed."

"How can a splinter do this?" Findley asked.

Kristofer smiled, thankful someone else had asked what he felt he could not, as he knew if he spoke up again, the tears would resume in force.

"Simply put, a splinter can't do this. A splinter would only damage the part of the body it entered." the doctor smiled as she replied. "But if the splinter carried germs or bacteria, then it could have given Hamish a small infection." She then addressed them all. "You all must remember that a coma is not necessarily bad."

Kristofer wanted to scream at her. *How dare she say it wasn't bad!*

"It's the body protecting itself, to stop anything worse

happening," she continued. "Hamish is still fighting, you see? It's a good thing. Much better than him being awake while all of this is happening."

"How long do you think until there's a prognosis?" Simon asked—the voice of reason as ever.

"Hopefully, after the lab tests his blood tomorrow morning." The doctor then motioned with her hand to the exit. "You all should go get some sleep. You can come back here at midday and sit in the room with him. But for now, we must keep him monitored and in isolation for twelve hours."

"I can't leave him," Kristofer blubbed.

"But there's nothing you can do for him here," the doctor said in her best bedside manner. "If you are needed, we can call you. But being in here, in this waiting room, it doesn't do Hamish or you any good."

Kristofer knew it was the best call. He knew he should go home, but nothing in his body would let him.

Simon felt the same but was aware of the others in the room waiting with them. He turned to Amber. "I'll call you when we can visit him, okay? You best take them home."

Before Amber could reply, Findley addressed the doctor again. "I think he got it in Mike Fisk's house. We were there today. And that place is probably chockfull of disease. So, if he got an infection, it's gotta be from there."

"You went where?" Kristofer asked, aghast.

Amber turned to Findley with an angry expression. "Tell me you're joking."

"Didn't the Sheriff tell you?" Emmie asked sheepishly.

"No, he did *not!*" Amber tried to keep her voice down due to where they were. "He just said he gave you a ride."

Emmie turned to Findley with a look that said *Oh no.*

"I'm going to have words with our Sheriff Benson," Simon said sternly before turning to the doctor. "If he did get something from that man's house, will it be easier to find out what it is, knowing where he may have got it?"

"Not really, no," The doctor shook her head. "Not with the time we have to find an answer."

"Please, someone help me" were the words that woke James Tran from his nightmare. Having sweat through his pajamas, he tried to catch his breath as he sat in the low light of his bedroom. The images of his dreams still haunted him. He saw a small, lightless, grimy room in the basement of the Petrie house. The darkness inside seemed to undulate as if it was hiding something monstrous in its cloak of shadows. Pip was against one wall, tied up with chains. Filthy, bruised, crying, and calling out for help—calling out for *his* help. "James, help me!" he cried.

James knew none of this was real. He knew his nightmares were simply that, without any grounding. He knew it was only his mind creating it all.

But no amount of rationality would prevent him from doing what he felt he *had* to do.

Dressed in his thickest winter clothes against the night's freezing air, James rode his bicycle across the streetlight-lit roads to the other side of town, toward Cromwell Woods. Having sneaked out of his house, as he regularly did, James had abandoned the warmth and comfort of his bed. Without the slightest of noises or hesitation, he got dressed and left.

He had to know *for sure*. He had to see if Pip was held captive, as his nightmares had shown him in vivid detail.

On his journey, James did not see one other person on the roads nor any lights in the houses he pedaled by. He had expected to see some sign of life. He even rehearsed the excuse in his head just in case someone had stopped him. *My grandma called. She needs me over at her house. She has dementia. It's an emergency.* Though he had no grandma in this town, he had not considered what he would say if someone knew this fact already. Not that it mattered, he soon arrived outside the Petrie house without having once to slow down.

Propping his bike up against the lamppost a few houses down the street, James unclipped the battery-powered headlight from his handlebars and steadied himself. Only now did he realize he didn't know what to do. He couldn't simply break into the house, especially with Adam's mother in there.

As he stepped toward the Petrie house, he glanced down at the icy concrete and the surrounding frozen lawns, looking for clues and any sign of Pip. Using the dull streetlights to guide his way, he gripped the headlight tightly in his hand, his finger paused over the power button, ready to switch it on at any given moment as if it were a weapon of some kind. He had no idea what he was looking for. He only felt he had to *try*. He knew if he waited for Findley, Emmie, and Hamish, they would talk him out of this or increase the risks of getting caught and in a lot more trouble.

No, he would do this himself and tell them about it afterward. Little did he know Hamish was in the hospital, unconsciously grasping onto his life, and his friends were being driven back to Findley's house, having been sat in the waiting room, hoping for good news.

The windows in the Petrie house were dark. The shadows inside were thick and all-consuming. Slowly and carefully, James stepped over the lawn to the large living room windows. He glanced over his shoulder as he walked, the grass softly crunching underfoot, checking for anyone watching him—but no one was there. No one was awake.

As he got closer, he tried to focus on the inside of the curtainless room, but no light made its way inside from the streetlights behind him.

Taking a breath, James steadied himself and slowly lifted the headlight in his hand. A sour, metallic taste filled his mouth as a chill ran through him. He was not built to be a criminal. This was not like him, not like him at all—and his body made sure to alert him of that by flooding him with every nervous feeling at its disposal. But some things were more important than fear, more important than his safety.

"For Pip," he muttered as he switched on the headlight and shone it into the living room.

The dull white light blasted its way through the glass, illuminating a sideboard in its circular beam. As James moved this light slowly to the left, his teeth began to chatter. He did not know if it was nerves or the cold causing it, nor the time to care. He just stared into the window as the narrow beam spotlighted the parts of the living room it covered. A lamp. The sofa. A pile of magazines. There was not much else—

Movement.

Something from the corner of the room moved. He was sure of it.

With a jolt, James moved the beam in its direction. Convinced in that one moment he would see something. *Anything.*

But there was nothing.

Silence.

Stillness.

Switching off the headlight, James looked around wide-eyed, then behind him at the neighboring houses. No one was watching him still. No one was awake enough to care.

Stepping back onto the grass, James trod carefully as he walked around the left side of the building. He could see the window to the open-plan kitchen/diner ahead of him.

As he carefully stepped over the wintery lawn around the side of the house, he noticed a thin yellow mist spreading over the yard and lapping its way around the house. Looking down at this dreamlike smoke, he grimaced with worry. This mist seemed to be everywhere. It was too surreal not to be noticed.

With his thoughts now screaming at him to run, he used all his willpower to persevere on the mission. He *had to*, or he would never forgive himself.

As the light in his hand shone through the small window into the kitchen/diner, he did not notice the floor beneath one of the chairs at the table. He did not see the dark red stain in the laminate under the chair's wooden legs.

He moved the light beam around the room and soon felt a sinking feeling that this was simply a fool's errand. He would never admit it, but he would prefer to find nothing more than something. Though he could not believe Pip to be the kind of person to take someone's money and run, he would much rather that than the alternative he had now forced himself to investigate. Sure, he was here to find clues, but in all honesty, he had hoped to find none.

Walking around the back of the house, James was more concerned with looking in through the kitchen's rear sliding doors, at a second vantage point into the same room, than anything else. He didn't see the mist getting thicker and thicker around him.

With his patience running dry, and in silent frustration, James moved away from the rear doors and over to the next window along the back of the house—this one tall but narrow, leading into the hallway.

As his light shone through the glass, it illuminated some fabric. A stained and wet material that hung down. James grimaced as he saw the mud and filth all over it. He presumed it to be a curtain.

Then the fabric moved.

What he thought was a curtain *moved*.

Dread suddenly hit him like a freight train as he realized that this was not a curtain, but a nightgown.

He raised his light upward, as his breathing became more stilted with fear, and soon was met with the cruel face of Mrs. Petrie glaring down at him from inside her house.

She looked like she had been in the wild for days, foraging for survival. Her hair was matted, her nails broken, muddied, and bloodied. Her eyes were bloodshot, and she looked exhausted. Her skin was so pale it looked almost gray. A far cry from the woman he saw at the police station the day before.

Too afraid to move his headlight away from the terrifying woman behind the glass, James could only back away, horror-struck.

"Why won't he take me?" Mrs. Petrie spat her words

hatefully at him. The sound was slightly muffled behind the window as her warm breath fogged the glass. "I begged for *years,* and he came for *his friend* in *one night* but left *me!*" Her fury was horrifying to witness. Her eyes were like pinpricks of hate, bearing down on the terrified James.

His hand dropped the headlight slightly, dulling his vision of the horrifying Mrs. Petrie.

"Now *you're* here, and straight away, he's *back?* For *you? You* don't deserve it! He's *my* family. Not yours." Spittle flew from her mouth, hit the window, and dripped down the glass as she continued. Too angry to cry, her fury was insurmountable. She slammed the glass with the balls of her fists. "I waited for years. Years!" she shrieked.

James could not physically react to her. His mind raced with confusion until he managed to fearfully utter the word: "He?' Trembling, as the mist encompassed his legs, James gritted his teeth and silently convinced himself to run for his bike, to get out of there as quickly as possible.

But her following words made him pause.

"Adam, baby," she pleaded. "Please take *me,* not him."

The nervousness he had felt before now paled compared to the sheer terror now flooding his body. His whole being ran as ice cold as the night, as his pulse pounded in his ears. He glanced up at her and saw she was staring wildly out, though not at him, but at something *behind* him. Toward the tree line of Cromwell Woods. The dead woods.

"Please, Adam, take me too," she continued speaking behind him. "I miss you. *I miss you.*"

Standing at the end of the backyard, between two trees, stood Adam. Not looking a day older than the last time James had seen him in the classroom, many years ago. Though not out in force, the moon illuminated this boy brightly. In its light, his skin and hair seemed to be colored in the same bright gray as his frayed and stained clothing.

This boy stared back at James. Smiling. Silent.

"A-Adam?" James couldn't help but say quietly, more to himself than anyone else. "No... It can't be."

Before he could process his thoughts, as the pleas of Mrs. Petrie continued behind him, he noticed there was also something standing beside this boy between the trees. A dog. A spaniel. A spaniel that stared back at him the same way Adam did, smiling as Adam did.

Bixley?

"Please!" Mrs. Petrie demanded as she frantically banged even louder on the glass.

If he had thought about it, he would have never taken his eyes off the impossible vision at the end of the backyard, but the noise forced his action.

As he glanced back, he saw Mrs. Petrie push herself away from the glass and disappear into the darkness of her house.

Spinning back toward Adam, James reeled as both child and dog stood much nearer to him. Now halfway across the lawn. They were in the same positions, still with the same smiles. They seemed as if they were made of stone and then picked up and placed nearer.

Now about ten yards away from the house— Their advance seemed impossible and unreal. James screamed as he stumbled backward.

Instead of falling or hitting the house, his back collided with something else.

Turning his head back in a shot, he was met with the

same smile but on a different person—someone he had not expected to see there.

Pip.

With the same gray motionless look of Adam and Bixley, Pip looked ethereal in the moonlight.

"Hello, James," Pip said, in a dream-like monotone.

Before James could reply, Mrs. Petrie wailed as she barreled out of the kitchen door toward them.

"*Take me!*" she yelled in fury. "I waited years for you. I gave you a friend. And you leave me?"

In unison, the dog, Adam and Pip turned their heads toward her. Their smiles suddenly grew wider and wider and wider and wider still.

Finally summoning the courage, James managed to scramble away from these things, in the direction of his bike. But as he ran, he could not help but glance back over his shoulder.

"*Take meeee!*" Mrs. Petrie screamed as she flung herself at the apparitions, crying loudly.

A second later, Bixley, Adam, and Pip's smiles grew to the furthest points of their heads. As their lips reached their apex, drool poured over their teeth and down their chins, and their heads opened backward simultaneously. The tops of their skulls levering widely back, as if on command. Long, thorny vines then burst out of their exposed throats like sharp and brutal tentacles.

As he screamed in horror, James could not hear Mrs. Petrie's last words.

"*Thank you! Thank you!*"

James caught sight of something else within the tree line as he reeled away from the attack.

Despite the tears in his eyes, he could see many other

figures standing in the mist. At least a dozen other dark-shrouded people. From where they stood, a clacking rattle sound echoed. It was a horrible and foreboding sound, like hundreds of rattlesnakes lying in wait.

As these rattles grew louder, as the silhouettes in the woods still watched, James glanced back at Adam, Pip, and Bixley.

He could not fathom the horror he then witnessed.

He could not understand what they had done to Mrs. Petrie, who lay dead on the grass in a crumpled and bloodied mess as the mist drifted over her.

As Pip and Adam's mouth vines flailed and rattled, they began to turn away from the dead Mrs. Petrie and look toward James. As they turned, their legs remained stationary. They inched in his direction as if they were gliding on ice. Snaking forward in a serpentine fashion, slightly left, then right, but always forward.

James did not remember running from the house or getting on his bike. He remembered none of his frantic scramble home. He only remembered standing outside his back door, escaping whatever he had witnessed at the Petrie house. He wept in relief and horror as he stood holding the door key.

THE JOURNAL

F indley had no idea anyone was in his house, let alone waiting for him to emerge from his bedroom. Still in a sleepy daze, he padded down the stairs barefoot, his eyes tired and half open. It was only when he saw Emmie, still wearing her pajamas from their sleepover, standing in the hallway speaking to Binh and Kathy Tran, he remembered all that happened late last night. The hospital visit. Hamish's coma.

With a worried look, Emmie looked up the stairs at Findley. "It's James," she said.

Immediately Findley's thoughts - *James is dead.* His face went slack with shock.

"He won't come out of his bedroom," Binh added.

The shock soon turned to confusion as Findley reached the base of the stairs and looked at both James' parents and then Emmie. "James," he began to say before pausing for a few beats. "...won't come out of his room?"

Amber, Findley's mother, walked out of the living room and smiled at her confused son. "Good, you're awake," she said. "Get dressed. You and Emmie are going over to see James."

Findley was more than confused. After a friend went missing and another fell into a coma, anyone wanting to stay in their room seemed inconsequential to him and *more* than understandable. "You want me to go over to James'," he asked in a monotone. "And get him to come out of his room?" he looked at his mother. "Really? That a thing now? Maybe he wants to sleep?"

Amber shook her head, not wanting to extend this conversation. "Please, go upstairs and throw some clothes on." She said, then turned to Emmie. "You too, dear."

With a disbelieving shake of his head, Findley strode back up the stairs to his room, closely followed by Emmie.

"Thank you," Kathy Tran called up after them.

"It's all gonna be fine," Findley heard his mother say quietly to the Trans.

Before he opened his bedroom door, Findley heard Kathy reply to his mother, her voice almost too soft to hear.

"I'm so worried," Kathy said. "He won't stop crying."

Findley and Emmie turned to each other as they walked into his bedroom. Without words, they knew each other felt the same... That this was strange. That *all* of this was almost too weird to be real life.

JAMES SAT on the edge of his bed in his pajamas. Next to the bed on the floor, the pile of clothes worn late last night sat in a discarded heap. He stared at the blank wall opposite when Findley and Emmie opened the door to his bedroom and walked in. Without turning to greet them, James' stare remained stoic and unmoving. His cheeks were stained with tear streaks, and his eyes were red.

"Hey buddy," Emmie said kindly as she sat on the bed beside him.

Findley walked to the other side of the bed and propped himself against the window sill. "Your mom's worried, bud," he said, trying to ignore James' obvious emotional state, choosing instead to talk to him as if it were any other day. "They said you're adopted, and they want you to leave and find your birth parents. Apparently, they are carnies or something."

James couldn't help but exhale a quick laugh as Findley's joke cut through the heavy atmosphere like a razor. Though his smile was pained, James turned to Findley. "You're an ass," he sniffed. He tried to control any more tearful emotions threatening to break through again.

"I am," Findley smiled back.

"So, what's up?" Emmie asked kindly, putting one hand on James' shoulder.

James first checked the door to make sure it was closed. He knew his parents were outside, so he replied to his friends under his breath, out of any potential parental earshot.

"I saw Pip," he began, recounting his late-night excursion to the Petrie house. As he spoke, Findley and Emmie's worry turned to fear as they hung on every word. Without even a moment of disbelief, they each took every word as gospel. No matter what was said. Adam Petrie, Pip, the trees. The vines. The horror. The deathly fear.

When he finished, James reached down and picked up his winter coat from the floor. Turning it around to his friends, he showed them the back of the thick fabric. Protruding from it were a dozen long, thin pieces of wood. Each was embedded in the material, but not so deep they could pierce his skin. Splinters.

"What the flitsticks are they?" Findley exclaimed as his eyes widened.

Emmie also stared, slack-jawed.

"I dunno," James shrugged. "I think I was lucky I had my big coat on. They were stuck all over my back when I got home. Must have been shot at me."

"Shot?" Emmie asked. "Like with a gun?"

"I dunno," he said as he dropped the jacket back to its resting place on the carpet.

"No wonder you wanna stay in bed," Findley said with a sigh as he sat on the bed opposite James.

The three friends sat in silence for a moment, each contemplating what to do next.

Findley eventually muttered, "So, Pip...he's gone?"

It was only after those words were said that it truly hit home for the three of them—even James. The reality of their friend not coming back. That whatever he was now was not the same person they knew, and that he was somehow part of everything that was happening to the town.

"It wasn't him," James said. His voice—though upset—was whispered to avoid his parent's hearing. "Sure it looked like him. But it wasn't. It was... Evil. I felt it. Just evil."

"What do we do?" Emmie asked.

James wiped his nose on his pajama sleeve and looked at his friends. "We gotta get help."

Findley thought for a moment, then turned to James. "Help?" he asked. "From who?"

"We gotta speak to Pip's mom," James said sheepishly. "She was right. She was very right."

Excerpt from the Journal of E Eagleton – January 20th, 1943

THE BOSS DRAGGED me aside this morning, sat me down, and told me all about the Cromwell Woods. Well, what he thought about the Cromwell Woods, and what his old boss had told him.

Called it a 'rite of passage,' whatever the hell that means. I had no idea what to say to him. I know it's been a doozy of a time with all those deaths, but what he said was insane. It had to be insane, right? Sure, the woods had died over the years, but this?

I gotta write it all down in case I forget what he said.

How can the trees be alive? How can they pretend to be humans? How can they make us see the dead? He threw all this stuff at me, and I can't wrap my head around any of it.

I joined the Sheriff's department to help people, and cos my dad was once Sheriff, but this other guy waits till I make my way up to Deputy to tell me that we're not here to help anyone at all, but to keep the balance. What the hell is the balance? I didn't join my friends fighting the Nazis for this?

I remember his words, more or less. 'You'll be Sheriff soon enough, same as your pops was, and you'll need to keep the secret 'cos you can't beat 'em. Your pop was lucky enough to never have to deal with it.'

Madness.

He blamed all those deaths in town on trees. GODDAMN TREES? Not even live trees. No. The freakin' dead ones in Cromwell.

Sure, we've found four bodies over the past couple of years. Each cut up like an animal would do. But instead of seeing that animal, searching the area for a bear or a wild cat, he got everyone to say that each one was either an accident, self-inflicted, or some other hoo-hah.

I got frustrated and asked if he was right, then how the hell so many people can live nearby and be ok? How can people walk through the woods and not get hurt? His reply was that they posed no threat.

They attack when attacked.

They attack when called.

They attack when you are afraid.

They attack when discovered.

If you don't engage with them or show fear, you remain safe.

If any of what he said was true, we can't ignore whatever is there. We have to fight them. Whatever they are. I can't be the only one that thinks this. I can't be the only one that won't roll over? But at the end of the day, I guess I didn't do the right thing or say the right thing. As the boss sent me home to 'cool off' for a few days.

"FINALLY DECIDED to listen to me, eh Matt?" Eddis Eaves-Eagleton said as he stared out the window overlooking the care facility parking lot. The midday sun was bright, making the whole town, even this asphalt parking lot look idyllic, though still mostly frozen.

Nearing his eightieth birthday, the old Sheriff of Hemlock Creek looked every inch of those years and more. Though his mind was sharp, his body had changed; changed for the worse. His skin was much looser, his muscles withered, his wrinkles exponentially more numerous, and his hair was only a specter of the once proud mane and long beard. "About time; I ain't got long left."

With a crisp white sheet pulled up around his chest, E squirmed in his bed, not feeling any comfort.

"I *always* listened to you, E. But back then, it was all too much to hear... Too much to believe." Sheriff Matt Benson replied as he sat on a chair beside the bed. "How are you doing anyway? They treating you alright in here?"

"How am I doin'?" E rolled his eyes. "You're kiddin' me?" Before allowing Matt to reply, E continued. "I've been stuck in this damn bed for years... All the people smile and talk nice, but only cos they feel guilty that I ain't standin' up and leavin' here any time soon, or ever again." He grunted. "They always want to wipe me down, make me move. But until the day I leave this old life, I ain't letting anyone... nurse, doctor, porter, *anyone* touch me, prod me, examine me. I *pay* them to be left alone." He nodded to a white water bowl on the cabinet next to him, with a washcloth hanging over its lip. "It's all I need. I'll wash my damn self. I'll check my own pulse. I'll shove the thermometer up my own ass if they need it. Besides, they can do what they want to me when I'm dead. Which ain't too far away. I can feel it creepin' up."

"Don't say that," Matt said with a sad smile. "You'll pull through. You always do."

"I don't *wanna* pull through," E looked at Matt intently. "I ain't got nothin' or no one to go back to, and I got Agnes waitin' for me on the other side. So, I ain't pissy about dyin'." He grinned. "I'm kinda lookin' forward to it. I miss her." He waved his hand up to Matt dismissively. "And I know, yeah, yeah, lots of people care about me here, blah blah... Well, I've seen behind the curtain enough times to get that this body's givin' up the ghost. Ain't no ending. Just another chapter of my existence."

Matt couldn't reply. He could only sit quietly.

"So, what changed with you, huh?" E asked, intrigued by the Sheriff's presence. "You told me was I was insane. You said I lost my mind. You didn't wanna hear that those woods were alive and they killed that boy?"

"Yeah, I did," Matt admitted with a sad smirk. "Now I'm more than happy to tuck my tail between my legs and ask for your forgiveness."

"How come?"

Matt took a moment to think before replying. "I can't see any other way to explain this stuff anymore," he said, "and it's happened *again*. But bigger this time."

"Bigger, how?" E asked, noticing the Sheriff was masking his fear. The same fear E had seen when Matt was younger and had escaped the woods with Sarah Charles.

"Adam Petrie's mother," Matt said matter-of-factly. "We found her this morning. In her backyard. Same deal as her son."

"Cuts and splinters?" E asked.

"Yet somehow worse." Matt nodded as he stared down at his feet mournfully. "I should have listened to you."

"Stop it!" E scolded, so much so that it caused Matt to snap out of his thoughts and look back up at him. "You had no idea what to do, did ya? You saw a kid. The kid had stuff all over him that made no sense to you. You couldn't find a way to say it, to explain it. So, you did what you did... You just made it so the town could carry on. We *all* did the same. Besides, what else were we gonna say? What good would it do, anyway? Just to tell the truth? This town would go into full-on panic mode. So, I get your reasonin', cos I did the same as you, for too long."

"I didn't even try to investigate any of it," Matt sighed. "I just swept it under the rug. You wanted to help me. You *knew* what it was. Maybe if I had listened—"

"Oh, you would've *not* been able to stop a goddamn thing," E interrupted. "And the worse thing is, no matter what I say, what I tell ya, end of day I know nada. Can't prove one bit of this... You can't arrest a tree, can ya? And you know what happens if you try and bring fire to that fight. Not that what your friend Gerry did was intentional.

But I told you what happened to me. I told you about the fires."

Matt nodded, knowing everything E said was true, no matter how much his common sense told him it was not.

"This ain't no human." E continued. "I don't think it's got a rational mind. I don't think it feels pity or hate. It just *is*. So, yeah, if you *did* listen to me, all you would have gotten is guesses in return. And what then? You close the woods to the public? You said that woman died in her backyard? *Not* in those woods, so would it really have made a lick of difference closing anything? What else could you have done back then?"

"Well, I'm here," Matt said, trying to appear less affected by all this. "And I'm listening."

"Everything's different since I last spoke to ya, ya get me?" E said, his voice losing any bluster. "I don't know how to say it all, but... realizin' you're gonna die? It lets you kinda remember life, if you get my meanin'? It's like a final gift the dark gives ya. It shows ya things you thought were long forgotten. Brings clarity to where there was none before."

"Forgotten?" Matt asked. "What d'you mean?"

"Like a whole world of memories," E spoke as he reached over to his bedside cabinet and opened the drawer. "It all floods back in dreams. First in pieces. Then it gets bigger and bigger. Faces, places, and times you forgot are now shown to you in the clearest of light. But only, it ain't no dream. You *know* it's true. You *feel* it's true." Bringing out a book from the drawer, leather-bound and tied with a buckle, E held it up to the Sheriff. "I've been writing it all down for a long while. Back from when I first saw it, everyone was off fighting that infernal war. But I've had to add a lot more to it recently; I see so much more now, you get me? Somehow, I knew you'd come, and I knew I *had* to finish this. Because I *have* to give it to you. You have to make sure everything is as it was and was as it is. And now you are here. With me sitting in this bed. I can feel the darkness. I feel it strong and focused."

"I'm sorry, I don't follow," Matt said, staring at the journal.

E smiled. "You won't get it. You never will, really. But you can ensure it's all right because there's *so* much wrong here. You see, it's all confusin' when we look at it like we do, it's all so convoluted, but really, in its simplest form, when you stand back, it's all logical. It's life. It's death. It's all one thing. I think... And like life and death, it's relentless, and brutal. Co-existence is the only way we have lived so far. Trust me, I tried it all. I tried to fight time and time again over the years, and nothing good came of it at all." He took a breath. "You gotta find the center. I believe *that's* where the truth is. It was a house made of the trees themselves, back in the day. May still be. But it moves. Never in the same place. You simply gotta follow the mist to the source. Took me a long while to realize it."

E's words confused the Sheriff as he took the journal the old man handed out to him.

"I tried to explain stuff when you took over the badge, but you had no way of knowin', No way of *seein'* the reality I was showin' ya. I was the same as you when I started. And not like it's happening every day."

"That's the thing," Matt said. "If it *was*, I could probably justify keeping my head in the ground. But it's growin' so much now. I can feel this'll go south real, real fast."

E's eyes widened as he painfully sat up in his bed. "What d'ya mean growin'? The woods are *growin'*?"

"I first noticed it when we did a helicopter sweep after the Reverend's boy went missing."

"I know about Pip," E said.

"You knew Pip?"

"A while ago, yeah. Poor kid. You don't really think he's a runaway, do ya, cos he ain't."

Matt shook his head. "I'm not *that* stupid; it's all too coincidental. But what am I gonna say? There's no body. All proof pointed to him running away. But he *was* at the Petrie house after we spoke to her. I saw how much of a bad, bad liar Mrs. Petrie was. I could *tell* she was hiding something, just couldn't prove it. Now she's dead, so we may never know, and like Adam Petrie, I couldn't go with my gut. Had to go with what was the most believable."

"And what did you see in the helicopter?" E asked. "What's made this so urgent?"

Matt smiled as he spoke, barely believing his words. "The woods. Over the last couple of weeks they've got bigger and bigger. Started with a few trees cuttin' in the dirt track at Edson Dam. I knew something was up as soon as I saw that, so I started tracking it, feeling it was not right."

"How big we talkin'?"

"We're talking huge." Matt met E's worried stare. "About fifty yards. Straight over the track and up the hill. Each day I go back there, new trees. Fully grown ones. Dead too, like all of the trees. How no one said anything or even noticed it is beyond me. Anyway, we're putting a barricade around the dam today. Stop people from getting near it without raising suspicion. I'm trying my best to keep a lid on it all. That's why I'm here."

"Well, I guess all bets are off then. I wish I could give you answers to solve this," E said, resting back in his bed. "*If* I had those answers, then all this would be different. But the book will at least tell you what I've seen. With the growin', though? I hope it ain't got a taste for killing."

"It can get a taste?"

"Maybe? Dunno... I thought it could be like a weed, you see? Some weeds' entire existence is spent extinguishing other plants it finds for no real reason. And those other plants have done nothing to provoke it. We could be those other plants. We could have just happened across it at the wrong time. Who knows how these messes start? But it sounds like that thing is changin', and I hope it ain't no weed, cos we won't stand a chance if it's gonna grow. I have a recollection it's some kind of thing, though. A flesh and blood thing. But..."

"What? A recollection?"

"Even though I remember so much more than I did, I also forget so much, you see?" E looked annoyed. "Death's a bitch, you know. It gives so much but takes even more away. That book ain't finished, though. I got a few more things to write. Which I'll do today, okay? You can come by tomorrow to get it. That good with you?"

"Sure thing... I wanna know as much as I can." Matt stared down at the journal. "And this, even if there's no silver bullet in what you wrote, at least will tell me stuff I didn't know."

"If you don't think I'm insane now, you *will* after readin' that." E smiled. "All I can think of to get through this is you *need* to keep it all in balance. If it's changed, growin', you gotta find a way to get through."

"Okay," Matt replied unsurely, then stood up. "For the

record, I don't think you're insane; I just think you're a grumpy ol' bastard, that's all."

E suddenly let out a deep belly laugh. One that made him wince and deliver a dreadful-sounding, lung-rattling cough. "Come by tomorrow," he reiterated.

THE CAR RADIO buzzed with static as Sheriff Matt Benson picked up the receiver from the dashboard.

"Yeah, I'm here. What ya need?" he said after clicking the button on the handset.

Sitting in the police issue vehicle outside the care facility, with E's journal resting on his lap, Matt looked very tired. He had read pages upon pages of the journal while sitting in his car, his thoughts whirling. The weight of the day, the weight of the week, had got to him. Even though the clock displayed 11 am, he was more than ready for bed.

"I got something, boss," the voice of Deputy Shaun Williams came over the radio. "Thought you'd wanna know about it ASAP."

Matt closed his eyes, dreading what the Deputy was about to tell him. "Yeah, what is it?" he sighed.

"Was doing my check at the hospital," the Deputy explained. "There's a kid called Hamish Flynn there. He was admitted late last night."

"He's in the hospital?" Matt almost shouted his question in shock. "What the hell? Why?"

"He's in a coma."

Matt stared out of his windshield, feeling at a loss.

The deputy continued on the radio, "You told us to let you know if we found anything strange, and this is *really* strange."

"How's it any more strange?" Matt asked, dreading the answer.

"They pulled out thirty-two long bits of wood from all over his body. Docs can't explain how he got 'em. That strange enough for ya?"

Excerpt from the Journal of E Eagleton – September 14th, 1943

I DON'T KNOW what to write.

I don't know what to think.

I saw him. I saw him with my own two eyes.

I didn't imagine it.

He stood there, as clear as day is bright. Smiling at me. Said nothing and just stared.

I was at his damn funeral only a week ago.

I saw his body.

The boss had died. Dead. Final.

He died so painfully.

I saw those bites.

I saw all that blood.

He was dead. DEAD.

Ignoring the vast gouges all over him, the coroner pulled out dozens of wooden barbs from all over his body. Too big to be considered splinters. They were like long sharp needles.

But somehow, tonight, he was there.

I'd gone that deep into those woods searching for that wild animal, as I did on all my days off. I had to find it. But I found that place instead. That house, if you can call it that. It was made of twisted trees. The branches made their own window frames and doors. It was like something out of a nightmare. As soon as I saw it, I felt my guts drop, but it got worse when he showed up in that doorway. Smiling as if he was waiting for me.

He was there.

Alive.

No damage to his body that he had in death. But he was wearing some filthy clothes.

He wasn't him, though. His feet. He didn't even have feet.

Long bits of tree stuck out from the bottom of his pants and went into the floor. I can't explain it right. But he was NOT human.

Then he smiled.

Oh, Jesus. That smile.

It was vast. It looked hungry.

His teeth were like little razors. Sharp and pointy.

He said, "It's not time yet." Then his whole damn head opened up.

I ran.

I'm not proud, but I ran.

I couldn't do this alone.

Managed to corral a posse of officers and other folks who knew there was something in Cromwell Woods. I couldn't tell them what I saw. I lied to each of 'em. I shouldn't have. My pops taught me better than that, but what else was I to do?

I told them all to bring gas. I had the idea that we needed to burn the forest down. Get rid of them all. For good.

But I was wrong.

I didn't listen to the boss when he warned me. Only reading back my writing now can I see how I could have avoided this.

We got so deep into the woods, but the house was gone. Vanished from where it was.

Then that weird fog came in. Lookin' like it was rotten. Surrounded us.

I gave the order to retreat and throw gas on every branch and bit of dead brush we passed. Soon the whole place stank so much of the gas fumes it was painful to focus.

It couldn't have been longer than a few seconds after we struck that match that it all went to hell. I'd never seen anything like it, nor do I think had anyone. I've seen some evil, but this... This was worse than anything I've ever seen, read or heard of.

The trees. They turned on us. Their branches shot out like spikes. Ripping. Tearing. All of them. Dragged 'em up into the air, pulling them apart.

And that face. That face in the trees...

Then they came. Those... other things. Not dead ones. But others. The shadow things. They all stood 'round watching as the trees attacked. I can't explain how or why or even what they are. But they just stood by as if to witness our massacre.

Me and fourteen people walked into Cromwell Woods to stop this all.

Only I survived it.

I don't know how I did.

I was right in the middle of that slaughter. Then something hit me. I was knocked out like a light.

When I came to, there was nothing around me except woodland. No bodies. No blood. No yellow fog. No remnants of carnage. NOTHING. Like it never happened.

I left those woods on my own.

I don't know how I lived when all those others died so viciously. With no bodies to bury and no evidence to show, no one would believe me if I told the truth. So, I decided quickly that my answer to the questions would be nothing. I would say that we were attacked, and everyone was taken. Don't know who by. But they had guns. I survived by hiding in the brush. Everyone else was not so lucky.

An awful lie, but better than me telling my truth then getting locked up for life in a padded room.

I don't think I'll ever forgive myself. I wouldn't know where to start.

As the Sheriff pulled up to the police station, he noticed a car in his designated parking space. Findley, James, Emmie, and Sarah Kaminsky stood beside it. They watched as Matt pulled up into the empty visitors' parking bay next to them. Each of those waiting carried the same expression. An expression that clearly said they had to talk to him, and he wouldn't like it one bit.

NO GOODBYES

As Sheriff Benson met the gaze of the four visitors sitting on the opposite side of his desk, his steely demeanor fell away. Putting up a front and lying was no use anymore, not when confronted by someone who knew him as well as Sarah Kaminsky did.

"Fine," Matt said. "But what do you want me to say?" he sighed as he glanced at Sarah sheepishly. "I did what I did for a good reason. Simple as that. I gotta say I'm not the bad guy here. I'm trying my best to keep everyone safe."

"And my son?" Sarah grimaced in reply, "what about *him*? Did you try your best with him too?"

Matt shook his head. "It's not the same, Sarah. Legally I can't just throw wild theories around to the public without any evidence. Phillip's bike—"

"Pip," Emmie corrected. "His name's Pip."

"Fine, Pip," Matt corrected. "His bike was also found by the train station, as you all know. There was zero evidence of foul play. So, what do you expect me to do? Besides, the investigation isn't even closed yet. His running away was simply the most *realistic* theory with the evidence at hand. It's not the definitive answer. There's still hope, you know?"

"No, Matt," Sarah said, fighting back her tears. "There's no more hope. That thing in Cromwell Woods *took* him. James saw enough to convince me last night." Sarah motioned to the seat next to her where James sat. "Ask him!" she said.

James squirmed in his seat.

"I'm sure it's not as bad as you think," Matt said as he turned to James. "What did you see, kid?"

"I..." James began. He looked at Sarah, then at his friends, before looking back at the Sheriff. His voice trembled. "I saw him. Pip."

Matt's eyes widened. "You did? That's fantastic." He looked at Sarah, who now wiped the tears that had slicked down her cheeks. "Right?" His smile fell as he saw that no one else looked happy about this. "What am I missing?"

Sarah closed her eyes as she spoke. "He saw Adam Petrie too. Just like when we saw Gerry." Her voice trembled with each word. "It was Pip, but not Pip. It was not Pip anymore. Not really."

Matt furrowed his brow and turned back to James. Despite the words sounding impossible, he believed them. He hid all surprise and his gut instinct to believe behind a policeman's poker face. "Adam Petrie?" he said. "You *sure* it was him, James? He's been dead for a while now, you know that, right?"

"I saw him and P-Pip...." James said. "I saw them both k-kill Adam's mom." Emmie put a hand on his knee in support as he continued. "They had trees coming out of their mouths, or... I dunno. I dunno *what* I saw. But I s-saw *them*. It was definitely them. They were so gray. So... P-pale."

Matt swallowed. The police had not made public what had happened to Mrs. Petrie yet. So, this boy knowing she was dead made what he was saying ring truer.

Findley leaned over to James. "Tell him about your coat," he whispered.

"Coat?" Matt asked.

James tried to steel himself, to explain what he had to,

but he was finding it all too complicated and terrifying. His body started to tremble.

Noticing, Sarah pulled the boy closer to her. Her maternal instinct commanded her to do so, despite her aching for her son's fate.

"It's okay," Sarah said, pushing aside her grief for one moment. "You don't have to say anything."

Emmie took charge, "They shot 'em as he ran away."

"Shot?" Matt's face fell in shocked confusion. "What the hell are you saying? Who shot?"

Emmie looked unsure. "Maybe not shot..."

Still trembling in Sarah's embrace, James reached into his pocket and brought out a folded napkin. He leaned forward and placed it on the table in front of Matt.

Matt discerned the shapes of long splinters protruding from the napkin's fabric.

"They were in the back of my jacket," James managed to utter.

With a pen in his hand, Matt opened the napkin on his desk with its nib, revealing the half-dozen long splinters.

"Jesus," he muttered. "They're the damn same."

"Same?" Emmie asked. "Same as what?"

Moving his hand to his intercom, Matt pressed its big red button and spoke into it. "Chloe, can you bring in the evidence from the Flynn case?"

"Sure thing, Sheriff," the female voice replied over the tiny speaker.

"Flynn?" Findley asked. "You mean Hamish?"

Matt nodded. "You're all aware of Hamish's current condition, right?"

The group nodded hesitantly.

"It was the splinter, right?" Emmie asked.

Matt nodded. "They're still running tests to see exactly what happened, but it wasn't *only* one splinter. Not by a long shot."

"How many?" Findley asked.

The office door opened, and a young officer, Chloe Dawson, walked in. She looked perturbed as she held out an evidence bag to the Sheriff. Matt took it without a word, then the Officer left, closing the door behind her.

"A lot," Matt replied as he opened the clear evidence bag and tipped its contents out. Falling from its clear plastic, three long splinters fell to the wooden desk. "I asked them to keep aside a couple for evidence."

Picking up one of the splinters from James' napkin and one from his evidence bag, the Sheriff held the two up side by side.

Both shards were almost identical.

"They the same?" Findley asked.

Matt reluctantly nodded. "Seems so."

Emmie's mouth hung agape.

"Are you going to arrest Mikey then?" Sarah asked. "He did that to Hamish. He must have been there last night as well."

"Was it him? Or the trees? Or Adam and Pip?" Matt asked, more frustrated than annoyed at the question. "We can't go and arrest Mikey, not when we don't know what's going on. And you're all just assuming Mikey is somehow at fault. But he wasn't there last night, was he, James?"

James shook his head.

Matt shrugged. "I don't know what any of us can do here. I'm the law, and I've no clue what we're supposed to do. What do I say about these?" He waved the splinters at them. "Huh? And what about Pip?" He motioned to James.

"About what you saw? I can't simply arrest Mikey 'cos of Hamish. There's no proof. Nothing. Even Hamish said nothing happened in Mikey's house. And I gotta be able to tell everyone something *real*. Something concrete. Something they can fathom. Something provable—"

"Why does it matter what you tell anyone?" Sarah interrupted, annoyed. "This is bigger than that. This isn't about your job. You can put Mikey in a cell until he talks."

"That's not how this works," Matt protested. "I got to follow procedure. I might be Sheriff, but every person in this building has to follow the law. Or it's gonna get a lot worse."

"How can it get worse?" Sarah asked with painful rage. "Pip is gone!"

"Listen to you all. You say Pip and Adam, or whatever you saw, shot these splinters at James, right?" Without waiting for confirmation, he continued. "Then you want me to arrest Mikey cos you *think* he had something to do with it, despite having no idea. You do realize there's no logical sense here?"

As Sarah opened her mouth to talk, Matt raised his hand to silence her. "Let me finish," he said. "I'm not saying I don't believe you. Cos trust me, I do. It may have taken years to finally admit it, even to myself, but I know there's something in those woods. I know some things look like the people we know. I know it takes people. But I can't act on vague presumptions. I can't. Period." He continued and looked at each of the four in front of him. "I *will* help you as you will help me. Hopefully, we can figure it all out. But it has to be based on facts. *Evidence*. You understand?" He took a breath. "You can believe what you want about me, Sarah," he said almost apologetically. "You can blame me for Gerry. You can blame me for Adam Petrie. You can blame me for Pip. You can blame—"

"I don't blame you," she interrupted. "I'm just angry you left me looking crazy all these years. You *know* what happened to us. You know what happened to Adam Petrie. Only Mike believed me, and he...." She swallowed hard as she continued. "I don't know what happened to him... And Pip? I was going to blame you for him... But after what James saw." She nodded to the splinters on the table. "After seeing these... I know my boy is gone. I know Mrs. Petrie knew what happened." She motioned with her hand to Findley. "And he told you she smiled at him after he confronted her. I get it, *you* didn't see it, and I can't blame or hate you for that. But I, *we*, need you to believe us now. To help us. And we need you to stop thinking about what lies you can say to cover this up and start thinking of ways to stop this from happening to anyone else."

"It's not covering up... I'm trying to fix it," Matt replied. "I really am. Same as this town has always done. You may not see it, but it's the truth."

"Always?" Emmie said. "How? What d'you mean?"

"It's not only me. This is how we keep everyone safe. We try to figure it out in private without creating mass panic, cos panic means more people would be hurt." Matt sighed. "I went to see E, Sarah."

"E?" Sarah replied, visibly surprised. "Sheriff Eagleton?"

"Yeah. He gave me this." He motioned to the leather journal on the desk before him. "I think you should read it, too."

"What is it?" Findley asked, peering at the journal.

"A diary of everything that's been seen about the woods

by him." Matt put his hand on the journal. "He said it doesn't have answers but may help. I've read some. It's wild stuff. I don't know how much is real and how much is just... I dunno."

"Who's Sheriff Eagleton?" Emmie asked Findley under her breath. He shrugged, as confused as she was.

"The Sheriff before me," Matt answered.

Emmie reached out to take the journal, but Matt kept his hand on it firmly as he looked at her, then at Sarah. "I think only *you* should read this, Sarah. This is not for—"

"I know we're just kids to you," Emmie cut in, "but we've seen a lot. And we *believe* what we see. We know more about all this than you do."

"They came to me and told me all they found out without hesitating," Sarah joined in. "And unlike you, they told me without any B.S... They were the only ones who saw Mrs. Petrie lying about Pip. *You* didn't listen. They told me all they've found out or seen about the woods. They told me about Mikey and what they think *he* did to Pip. Again, *you didn't listen.* They told me about seeing Pip without caring about how they sounded. They're hiding nothing. So don't you try and cut them out of this."

A knock on the office door caused Matt to feel relief, grateful for the interruption to this conversation.

Through the glass, looking deadly serious, Deputy Shaun Williams waved to Matt to come out of the room.

Matt removed his hand from on top of the journal and pushed it across the desk, closer to Emmie.

"You'll help?" Findley asked with a hopeful smile.

"I have a feeling if I don't, you four'll get yourselves in trouble."

Matt stood up and walked around his desk. "You all

read that, and we can try to figure this out. But the first sign of danger, I'm stepping in. None of you can be in harm's way. Understand?"

"Bit late for that," Emmie quipped.

Matt opened his office door, then spoke to the Deputy.

"I got some bad news, boss," the Deputy spoke as the office door closed.

Neither Findley, James, Emmie nor Sarah heard what was said outside the office between the two police officers. They were too busy staring curiously at the journal on the desk.

"Mrs. Kaminsky?" Findley said softly.

The still visibly upset Sarah looked at him with a pained smile. "Yeah?"

"There *is* still hope... Just because James saw what he saw doesn't mean Pip is gone. We don't know anything for sure. Your gut feelings might be all wrong about it."

SHERIFF MATT BENSON sauntered down the dim corridor of the care facility he was in only hours before. His skin was now sallow under the neon strip lights, made all the unhealthier by his dejected and mournful expression.

Having left Sarah, Findley, James, and Emmie with the journal, he couldn't help but feel letting them in was a mistake. Putting a grieving mother and three children in danger was stupid by all rational thought, but what else could he do?

Approaching the director's office, Matt paused for a moment. He gathered his thoughts before gently rapping on the frosted glass door.

"Come in," came the old male voice.

Opening the door, Matt stepped inside the office to be met with the kind face of Dr. Lakeland Turner, manager of the care facility and city morgue—Sarah Kaminsky's boss. Matt always found it odd the man in charge of a care home would also run the place they would all eventually go when they died.

"Sheriff," the old doctor said as he stood up from his desk, then extended his open hand across his desk.

Shaking hands, the two exchanged a polite smile before they sat down.

"I wish it were under better circumstances," the doctor said with genuine empathy. "You were friends, I believe, correct?"

"I'm not sure I'd go as far as friends. Not for years anyway, but—" stopping his words in their tracks, Matt then changed the subject. "Are you sure it's him? I was literally only here a few hours ago. He seemed fine. Happy even. Well, as happy as he could be."

"He was a salty ol' dog, wasn't he?" the doctor said, chuckling.

Matt attempted a polite smile, but the news hit him harder than he could have imagined.

"Would you like to see Mr. Eagleton?"

The doctor's question made his stomach lurch, but he could only answer one way. "Yeah, I think I would."

The walk from the Director's office to the basement-level morgue took only a few minutes. Still, it felt like an eternity to Matt. They walked in a somber silence, with the doctor leading the way.

.   .   .

As Emmie read the journal aloud to the others, they listened, enraptured. Having sat in the Sheriff's office for the better part of an hour, they had heard many tales from the journal of the woods. From times of war, all the way up to the account involving Sarah, Matt, Mikey, and Gerry.

"No fire, no guns, no ice, nothing we've tried has done a single thing except poke the beast," Emmie read aloud. "There's no way to know what will beat this thing, not without losing move lives, and we've lost more than enough already. Maybe it's time to get the town to move? Somehow just get everyone to leave, and give the land to... whatever it is that's there?"

"It's really not a bad plan," Findley said. "If you can't beat it, cheese it."

"Maybe it would die without us around?" Sarah asked.

Emmie turned the page.

Her eyes widened as she read the section on the next page. Immediately she looked at Sarah and half smiled.

"What is it?" Sarah asked.

Looking back at the page, she tried not to let any excitement be premature. "It's in big letters, underlined too." She read from the book. "Not all those taken are dead!"

Sarah smiled hopefully.

Emmie continued reading. "We had all seen Colton Buck taken away by the things in those woods. We also all saw him as one of those *things*. We all thought he was dead. We had thought that those gray versions of us were what we look like after they turn us... But they're not. We were wrong. After all this time, we now know they are not the actual people we see. They're..." Emmie paused and squinted at the word she tried to read. "Dopple...

gangers?" Emmie looked up, confused. "What the hell is that?"

"Copies," James said. "Doubles of us."

Emmie continued with a curious expression. "We found the house again; this time, it was on the far ridge by the Fairview Trail. It wasn't there before. But when we went out, it was right in the middle of the trail. Bold as brass. As if it had always been there. I went in, and... I don't know how to explain it. But in the wooden structure, time sorta slipped away. It felt like I was in there for a moment. As far as I knew, I peered in and then turned around to my officers, but according to them, I went in and didn't reappear for about ten minutes. They waited as long as they could and despite my ordering them not to, they were about to come in after me. But before they did, I fell out of the doorway. Holding Colton. He was alive. Not well, but *alive*."

"When was that?" Findley asked.

"1959," Emmie answered.

Findley turned to Sarah. "You think this Colton's still alive? Think we could ask him about it?"

Sarah shook her head. "I remember him. He died a few years back. His daughter runs the flower shop on Edgewater."

"It means Pip could still be alive," Emmie exclaimed with a new happiness in her voice. "*Probably* is alive."

"We *gotta* find that house," James said as he looked at Sarah hopefully.

THE THIN WHITE sheet had been lowered down to expose E's head. His expression was not blank like most corpses, but instead somehow content. More content than Matt had ever seen him. Not since E's wife was alive did he ever look so peaceful.

"He's finally with her," Matt said with a smile as he felt a tremble of emotion. "It's all he wanted." Taking him as much by surprise as the doctor. Matt cried. He didn't know why. He simply did.

For the moments the doctor gave him to grieve, Matt felt like he was crying not only for E but for all those he knew and lost and did not have a chance to mourn.

After a couple of minutes, as Matt sniffled the tears away, Doctor Turner smiled, then pulled out an envelope from his pocket. "After you left earlier on, Mr. Eagleton asked a nurse to take this envelope and ensure it was given to you."

"What?" Matt said as he took the envelope and stared at it. "He said he was gonna write me something. Told me to come back tomorrow."

Scrawled on the front of the envelope were the handwritten words, *Sheriff Dingus*. Matt chuckled as he read it.

He then looked over to the doctor. "He knew, didn't he?"

The doctor looked at the body with a smile. "Unlike most of us, Mr. Eagleton had a sense of when his time would come. I think he knew, yes." He looked at Matt. "It's a phenomenon that's widely recorded but never spoken about. He obviously wanted to tell you these things after and didn't want you to know before for his own reason. But I should point out, and this is just me being honest, he may have been suffering from some mental deterioration at the end. Kind of the early stages of his body shutting down. So I would suggest reading the letter with that in mind.

Written right before he passed, it may contain some substantial delirium."

Matt nodded, then looked at E as she spoke to the doctor. "Will there be an autopsy?"

"I don't think it is required here," the doctor replied. "His decline was recorded over the past few weeks; there was nothing suspicious about it. Quite expected, really. A few days earlier than I thought it would be, though."

"I had no idea he was *that* ill. He said he was, but... I thought he was just being E." Matt put his hand out and placed it on E's shoulder. "Say hi to Agnes for me, Chief," he said under his breath.

"We have left a box of his belongings in his room, should you wish to collect them." the doctor pulled the white sheet back over E's head. "I know he had no next of kin, so maybe you are the nearest thing?"

Matt didn't know what he could do with anything E may have left behind, but he agreed to take whatever there was anyway. The doctor was right. There was no one else.

As Matt's foot hit the first step to take him up to the second floor, he opened the letter from E.

MATT,

Okay, I admit it... I'm getting out of here before the fit hits the shan. But I'm glad my body won't let me go on anymore. I am <u>done</u>. I want out. I want to see Agnes.

I feel the darkness coming, and I'm not only talkin' about death. I think anyone who has seen what's really in those woods... Well, they're kinda attached to it from then on. I feel sick to my stomach any time I'm near those awful trees. And it's weird, but I feel that now. As soon as you left here, I felt it again.

*Like the goddamn wooden bastards were outside lookin' in. I feel
it so strongly. Like my guts are being pulled down to the floor.*

*Now, you may ask why I didn't say what I saw when you
were here earlier... Well, simple answer, I couldn't even begin to
answer the questions I know you'd have asked me. But here it is.
The point of the letter... And I cannot stress its importance...*

LET

HAMISH

GO

*I ain't got no time to go into specifics. But read those words
repeatedly. My life, your life, <u>everyone's</u> life depends on it.*

*You know when I pulled you back from fallin' in the dam
while we were trying to get Dave Hawkins off that ledge? Well,
if you don't do as I say, I won't be able to pull you back.*

So I say yet again... READ IT! UNDERSTAND IT! DO IT!

LET

HAMISH

GO

*Now take care of yourself, and see you on the dark side,
compadre,*

E

As Matt finished reading the letter, he felt a soreness in
his stomach and a stiffness in his bones, Heading into E's
old room, it felt like someone walked over his grave while
gut-punching him with a cannonball.

Folding the letter into his pocket, he could only
meditate on the doctor's advice to take the letter as possibly
delusional. Though he knew it was sensible advice, he also
knew E was firing on all mental cylinders when he visited
him earlier in the day.

How the hell did he know who Hamish was?

Before finishing the thought, he noticed a yellow mist coating the laminate floor.

"What the—?" Matt muttered as he turned the corner of the bedroom.

When he looked up, he gasped as his confusion spiked.

On the bed, lying as he did on the table in the care facility's basement, was E. Looking as dead as he had mere moments ago.

Matt tentatively took a few steps closer to the bed—his jaw agape.

The closer he got, the more real the impossible vision became.

Looking back at the door, Matt wondered if this was all a sick joke. He half-expected the doctors and nurses to be there, ready to shout, 'April fool!' at him. Not that it would make any sense, and nor was it even April.

He did not notice the mist start crawling up his legs.

He did not see the body of E lying on the bed, open his eyes.

He did not see the body on the bed sitting up.

He did not see the body on the bed facing him and grinning.

Matt was met with this horrible smile as he turned back from the door.

"Jesus!" Matt exclaimed as he took a step backward. His eyes were wide and focused on the impossibility in front of him.

"You come to visit me again?" E said with a leering, perverse, sadistic grin.

"What the hell is going on?" Matt almost shouted at E. "You're dead! I saw you *dead*."

"What is dead anyway?" E asked, his grin growing wider.

Matt knew this was not E. He knew this was not his friend.

E had said in the letter that his stomach lurched every time he was near Cromwell Woods; Matt had never it. Until now. Now he did. *Now* he felt it. And he did not know how he knew, but he just knew it was the same feeling E had mentioned.

"What are you?!" Matt said as he backed up further, side-eyeing the open doorway into the corridor.

"We are here for *you*," E said as his grin grew. "You have been *watching* us. You have been *interfering* with us. We want *you*. We want to feast on *you*. We want to grow through *you*."

The grin extended wider, but instead of this figure's mouth opening and exposing a collection of rattling snake-like vines, the skin on his face began to crack apart—like china. A minor fracture from the edge of his grin grew and spread over his face, then down his body.

Between these fractures, small vines began to protrude. Each of them held small pieces of the cracked skin that made up E's face and body on their tips. Hundreds of vines holding up hundreds of small parts that all together made up this apparition of E.

As the vines separated, so did E. His smiling body split apart with a squelch and a crack, and the pieces moved outward until his whole being was nothing except a collection of hundreds of twisting vines. Each was holding a small piece of his body on the end. There was no blood, as this was nothing but a façade.

The vines then flailed wildly and made a loud clacking sound as they reared upward.

Matt could see the vines had broken in from the outside through the wall at the base of the bed. Cracked straight through the building's solid brickwork.

As Matt backed up further, his back hit the wall. Still wildly lashing to and fro, the vines advanced slowly off the bed and toward him.

Then the hundreds of vine ends fused together again. The tiny patches of skin-like material on their tips that had made up E began to re-group, but this time into the form of someone else: the legless, naked body of Mad Mike Fisk.

With thicker vines raising up this false image, Mad Mike appeared to be carried amongst the living plant, not made up of it.

Then this Mad Mike smiled the same sickly smile E once wore.

"Why did you leave me in those woods, Matthew?" Mike said as a chuckle seeped out of his mouth.

Matt could not answer. He stared back blankly, his mind racing, wondering how to escape.

"This form was a glorious feast," Mike said. "We consumed him slowly over decades."

A scream from the open doorway made this monster turn with a sudden snarl.

Before the terrified Doctor Turner could turn and run, pointed vines shot out from under Mad Mike and flew at incredible speed toward him.

The doctor, though, did not see the same scene as Matt did. He did not see Mad Mike. He did not see any *person*. He only could only a collection of furiously flailing vines.

His brain could not decipher what was happening as a

dozen branches pierced his body like hot knives through butter, dragging him inside the room.

Holding the doctor like a rag doll, the clacking sound got louder as it pulled him into Matt's view.

In Matt's eyes, Mad Mike let loose a furious wail as his vines easily pulled Doctor Turner's body apart.

As the blood arched across the room, Mad Mike's fury disappeared, and his grin returned.

Without pausing, this monster advanced on Matt from above, like a serpent about to strike its prey.

"We will taste your decay!" Mad Mike roared.

Matt closed his eyes tightly, accepting any escape from this monster was unlikely and his demise was almost assured.

LIKE MAGNETS

Sarah was a mix of emotions. The thought Pip could still be alive filled her with a warm glow, but having just heard of E's passing from the Deputy, she also felt a strong pang of sadness. E was the man who had been there for her growing up. A man who had stood up for her. Protected her against the town's anger after the accident in Cromwell Woods. Anger they misguidedly aimed her way. A man who, more importantly, believed her, which is more than could have been said for her actual father, who sat silently by, unable to do much except say he was there for her.

She also felt a pang of intense guilt, as ever since she had her child, she had lost touch with E. Motherhood had taken over her priorities. Something she had done with all her friends. When she passed E in the town, she naturally stopped for a chat and exchanged banal pleasantries, promising to meet up properly very soon. And both knew this was merely a pleasantry, as each had their own lives now. She had even made an excuse not to go to Agnes' funeral, blaming it upon taking Pip to football practice.

She wished it would have been different. She wished she had made time for a man who did so much for her when she was younger and needed it.

The drive to her house was one of silence. Emmie was sitting in the passenger seat, still reading E's journal. Findley and James were in the back. Findley knew James was still terrified after what he had witnessed, so he sat close to him over the middle seat.

James stared out the window, watching the houses go by. He pictured Pip's face in his head, then the corrupted Pip with the vines flailing out of his Pez-head-like mouth.

As they pulled up to Sarah's house, they got out of the car, and she led them in. Emmie was flipping back and forth between three different pages in the journal with a curious look on her face as she walked through the hallway.

"Where's Mr. Kaminsky?" Findley asked Sarah.

"He's at work," Sarah said with a tinge of annoyance. "He said his church needed to show strength, not weakness, at a time like this." She shook her head and put the house keys in a bowl on a side table.

"It's all... what's that word... They're the same distance from each other," Emmie muttered, feeling a *eureka* moment as she marched over to Sarah.

"Equidistant," Sarah said.

"Equi-what now?" Findley peered over Emmie's shoulder, trying to see for himself, but he had no idea what he was looking at.

"What do you mean, Emmie?" Sarah said.

"You got a map of the town?" Emmie asked Sarah with a smile.

FIVE MINUTES LATER, they were all standing around Sarah's dining room table. A large map had been laid open in front of them.

With a pen in her hand, Emmie marked a circle on the large map of the town. Looking back to the journal, which was open to a page with a hand-drawn map on, she nodded to herself.

"This is where that house was in 1943," Emmie said as she flicked through the journal, looking for another page. Stopping at another map, she examined it carefully, then at the big town map. Leaning across the map, she marked another circle onto it.

"This is 1961," Emmie exclaimed as she repeated, looking for yet another hand-drawn map in the journal. Upon finding and examining it, she did the same as before and marked a circle on the town map corresponding to the journal map.

"And this is where it was in 1968," Emmie said, "when Sheriff Eagleton saw it, after what happened to you, Mrs. Kaminsky."

Sarah's eyes widened. "He told me he didn't find anything."

"Oh." Emmie felt like she had said something she shouldn't have. "He wrote about it in here if you wanna read?"

Hesitantly, Sarah moved over to Emmie and looked down at the journal.

"It's not much," Emmie said as she turned the page for Sarah, showing her the journal entry she was referring to.

Excerpt from the Journal of E Eagleton – December 14th, 1968

I'M EXHAUSTED.

Trying to corral a town that is thirsting for revenge when you can't tell them the truth is too much. Too difficult. Too damn annoying to handle.

We swept the woods looking for clues, making sure we

didn't take weapons or anything that could provoke whatever it was. And that worked as it always did. Not that my men understood a thing. They thought they were looking for a wild animal that killed a kid. Still, I convinced them that batons and pepper spray were enough, that if there were animals out there looking for blood, they would be in packs, and loud noises would draw more to us. Complete hogwash, of course. But they ain't the brightest of sparks. Good people, just a bit simple, that's all.

We found nothing, of course. The woods were only woods. Ugly dead woods.

No trace of Gerald Levy, no trace of Michael Fisk's legs. No trace of anything.

Well, that ain't <u>exactly</u> true.

We found nothing that could help us or the case.

One of my men found the house. That house. Again, it was in a place where it wasn't before.

And my men, being brave idiots, wanted to go inside.

I knew better than to go in unprepared. I said we would regroup and come back. We needed rope. I wasn't letting anyone go in there unless they were tethered. I went in, and it went belly up. I lost time. I can't chance more stuff like that happenin'.

So we left. Then after we tooled up, we went back in. Naturally, the house was gone.

My men quickly believed that we must have got lost and the house was somewhere. So I feigned confusion, and we searched the woods till sundown. I knew it was gone but couldn't say anything.

In the end, we said that nothing was found, I told my men to forget about the house. It wasn't part of the case. They weren't all happy about it, but they obeyed.

And the town didn't take too kindly to the news of us finding *no animal but soon forgot about it and went on with their lives as they seemed to always do.*

I went back to the woods a dozen or so times since. But I still couldn't find that house. I can only hope that the Levy boy is in there. Just like Colton Buck. Maybe I can find him.

But if the house stays hidden. I hope he is dead. Cos that house ain't no place to be.

EMMIE POINTED to the three circles she had drawn on the town map. "Look," she said as she put a dot in the center of the three circles. "This is the center."

From that dot, she drew three lines to each circle representing where the houses appeared. "These are all the same distance from here, get it now?"

Findley and James looked on, both not really understanding, but Sarah couldn't help but smile.

"You are a genius, you know that, right?" Sarah said, putting an arm around Emmie, smiling still at the map.

"She's definitely the brains," James added. "But all that, it's all just a guess?"

Emmie shrugged. "Good a guess as any."

"You're the brains, Em. I'm the looks," Findley joked.

Emmie pulled an ugly joke face at him in retort.

"May I?" Sarah took the pen from Emmie and leaned over the map. She drew around the three points on the map, with the anchor still at its center. Creating a line on which all three points sat. "It can't be a coincidence that it appeared to E so exactly placed like that, so the house must be at any point along this line?" She pointed to the circle she had drawn. "So if we go here and follow this path around, the house should be there, right?"

"I...," Emmie said. "It's only a guess, as James said."

"And why are we sure Pip'll be there?" James asked as he stared at the map.

"What if it was you?" Findley replied. "You'd want us to try, right?"

"We need a plan, though," James said. "We can't just go in there ."

They all fell silent, knowing they were all out of their depth.

Sarah glanced at her watch. "I think you guys need to get home. It's nearly 5 pm. Let's regroup in the morning. I'll go now and tell Matt—the Sheriff—what we found, okay? Maybe he can send his men into the woods to find Pip instead of us? I don't want any of you in danger, and I don't want Pip out there another night alone."

Findley turned to James, "Let's go to Hamish's and get an update from his dads, okay?"

Emmie picked up the journal. "Can I take this for tonight?" She asked Sarah. "I wanna read more of it."

Sarah nodded with a smile but was distracted by the thought of Pip alive and still trapped. She had trouble concentrating. "I don't think Matt would mind." She feigned a smile. "He's not a big reader."

HAMISH'S EYES OPENED.

Staring at the ceiling above him, he felt an emptiness like hunger, but not only in his stomach. The feeling was in every part of his body.

He did not remember when he woke up, where he was, or how he got there. He just knew he had to get on his feet. He had a feeling. A dreamlike feeling.

The walk through the hospital passed like a blur. This late at night, there was little staff around. and none of those still on duty saw Hamish walking out of the doors and into the freezing night air.

Sitting in the waiting room, his dads were too involved in their grief to see their son walk past the window in a daze.

Hamish did not know where he was going, but his body seemed to.

He stared down as his legs walked step after step, off from the street's asphalt and onto a grass verge.

His hospital gown should not have been enough to protect his body from the cold air, but the chill seemed distant to him.

He didn't feel the rock slicing open the base of his foot as he stepped on it. Even if he did, he did not think he would have cared. He allowed the feeling to take over him. Like a drug, this trance made him feel nothing but calm.

As the wind whistled past his ear, it sounded to him like a symphony of nature.

Hamish did not know what was happening.

But at that moment, Hamish didn't even know who he was or where he was.

THE POLICE STATION was abuzz as Sarah walked in and up to the reception desk. Everyone in there looked in a panic.

She stood by the desk, waiting for someone to come up to speak to her. She glanced around, looking for Matt, but she did not see him among the other officers. His office lay open and empty, with the light off.

She had no idea what was causing this furor. She could

only hear snippets of panicked conversations between the Deputy and other officers.

"The whole damn wall was ripped out."

"We found blood."

"There were branches everywhere."

"Keep trying on the radio!"

Sarah didn't see Officer Chloe Dawson walk up to her. Her eyes were wide and nervous as she tried to regain her police officer cool and calm demeanor.

"Hi, Sarah," she said, her expression slightly manic, catching Sarah off-guard. "I'm afraid it's not a good time."

"Where's Matt?" Sarah asked, sensing something was very wrong here.

"He's..." Chloe replied with trepidation as she looked around before lowering her voice. "We don't know where he is."

"What?" Sarah went cold hearing those words.

"He went to that care home on Willowbrook but didn't check in," Chloe explained as she kept an eye around her, ensuring no one heard her talking. "We sent an officer there to see what was up. They found the Sheriff's car, but not him, and inside... There was... I can't explain it, really."

Sarah didn't know how to reply to any of this.

"People heard all this noise coming from a room. The whole place was destroyed when we got there, and there was a big hole in the wall." Chloe's words trailed off. She could not believe any of this herself. "I'm sure he's okay. He *has* to be okay. He's the Sheriff."

MATT FELT a warm wetness on his back.

A pain rang through him, causing him to wince as he opened his eyes.

With his hands on either side of him, he pushed himself up to a sitting position, and it was only then he felt the strangeness of the surface he found himself upon. It was not solid, and it felt like an expanse of meat. Warm. Fleshy. Undulating.

The darkness around him was all-encompassing.

The stench there was... familiar. The smell of waste and rot and decay. Like Mad Mike's house times a thousand.

Though he could not see it and had no idea where he was, he horribly imagined lying amongst the congealed mass of a thousand corpses.

Am I dead? he thought.

"No, Matty," said a voice from within the darkness, hearing his thoughts. "You're not quite dead yet. Soon, but not right now."

With a gasp, Matt looked ahead, staring blankly into the pitch black, to where the voice came from. He didn't reply though, he just kept silent.

He reached down onto his belt, and to his surprise, he felt the butt of his pistol still in its holster.

"Won't do much good against them, ya know?" came the voice again.

Like the smell, the voice was also familiar, but he could not quite place it. He reached for the pencil flashlight from his breast pocket.

"Before you use that, I gotta warn ya," said the voice, "there's a lot of death in here."

Still staring ahead—still unable to see a thing—Matt flicked on his flashlight, aiming its beam straight toward the voice.

Sat, perched a few feet ahead of him, was someone he never thought he would see again. Gerry Levy.

Looking as ghostly gray as he had seen before. His eyes were dull and slightly milky. They did not wince when the light shined on him.

"Boo!" Gerry smiled.

Unable to respond, barely able to breathe, Matt scrambled away from this boy until his back hit a large wall —a sizeable meaty wall with the same consistency as the floor. On instinct, he aimed his flashlight around. Though there were no piles of corpses like he had imagined in his worst fears, what he did see what more surreal and kind of more terrifying; The floors and walls may have seemed like wood at first glance, but they had a fleshy texture. It was as if the wood itself had lost its solidity, turned squishy, and had been colored a blood red. It may not have been rotting corpses, but it was still horrific and confusing.

He then noticed the bones.

The many, many, *many* bones.

Not lying-in piles but embedded in the very floors and walls themselves. Bits of skulls, finger bones, leg bones, ribs. Not in complete skeleton form, rather separated into many different pieces.

As well as these many bones, the walls and floor were littered with hundreds of vines snaking all over the floor as if holding the very fabric of the horror together.

"You're wondering where you are, aren't ya, hoss?" Gerry asked.

"Who are you?" Matt spluttered, barely able to believe his eyes.

"I'm not Gerry if that's what you're thinking," came the reply. "Well, I am. Kinda."

"What the hell are you saying?" Matt's tone turned angrier. "*Who are you?*"

"Chill ya britches," the boy said. "I'm not *the* Gerry. But I'm the Gerry you carry with you and the one that died here."

"What does that even mean?" Matt reached for his holstered pistol.

"In here, when you die, you become part of all this," He motioned to the room around them. "Everything you know. Everything you are is absorbed into the walls, the floors. All of it."

Matt glanced around the horrific room. His flashlight shone upon each wall, and each looked the same—a meat-like wood with bones within it, held up with vines.

"Where am I?" Matt asked under his breath as he unbuttoned his holster.

"In a house. I think. I only know what I knew until I died, and I think I remember a house just north of the woods where we were." Gerry moved from the perched position to a seated one.

Matt, in an instant, drew his gun and aimed at the boy, keeping the flashlight pointed where he aimed.

"Let me out of here, or I'll shoot you dead." He commanded. "Don't test me."

"I'm dead already." Gerry held his palms up in appeasement to Matt. "But I'm not the *thing*. I'm still the remnants of *me*. Damn, I guess I'm not explaining it right."

"You only got a few seconds to try," Matt said sternly, his gun still aimed at the boy's head.

After thinking for a second, Gerry nodded to himself. "Okay. This place? It's like a stomach. Whatever is here, like me and many others, will die. Get it? But as you're dying, this *stomach* feeds on you. So when you die, you *combine* with it sorta."

"How did you die?" Matt asked.

"It's not the point," Gerry shook his head. "What made me, *that* is right here with you. Like a soul, I guess? Even if my flesh isn't around. Now you have come, and your memory of me connects with *that* part of me that's still here. Understand?"

Matt did not.

Gerry thought for a moment. "Then I'll put it this way. There are two kinds of people: the ones you know and those you don't."

Matt stared back.

"Right, and of the ones this place took. How many do you know personally? Not just their name?"

"Only you," Matt replied.

Gerry smiled. "And how many that you know of but don't actually know?"

"One, maybe two more."

"Exactly!" Gerry smiled happily. "And you *only* see me here! That's because what's left of me in here, and what you know of me, it's created what you see—"

"So what?" Matt snidely remarked. "I'm hallucinating? From a magic tree?"

Gerry laughed. "Kinda, but no more magic than what we did in science class. You remember when we did the hydrogen explosion thingy? That explosion wasn't there before. But the two things made it happen. But the other ones that came here, you *didn't* know. So you can't see or hear them, but they are here."

"Wait. You remember science class?"

"No, *you* do. So I do too." Gerry motioned to the room.

"This place, with all that was me being part of it, plus your memories of me? Then your brain sees me. Hears me. I am what you remember but also what I was."

"How long were you here?" Matt asked, believing what was said, no matter how confusing, though keeping his aim. "Before you died, I mean."

"No idea," Gerry shrugged. "It hurt. It hurt for a long time. Then nothing. And you can put the gun down. It won't do anything to me. I'm not here. You can't kill what died long ago." He pointed to a section of the floor next to him.

Matt's aim and flashlight turned to where Gerry pointed—to the white object protruding from the floor.

"That's one of my bones, dunno which though," Gerry said, smirking. "I think I counted thirty or so different people around here when I was alive. But I didn't have a flashlight like you do. I did have my lighter... Once. But that went out fast. So, I had to feel it by hand. *That* wasn't fun, I tell you that for nada."

Slowly Matt lowered the gun. "So, why are you here?"

"There's no reason. It just is. Just like this thing. Whatever it is, doesn't *decide* to do anything. It only does what it does." Gerry put his hand down and touched his skeleton. "Like a tiger eats another animal not out of hate or spite or evil or good. It simply needs to survive. Same thing here. It consumes. Again and again."

"That's crap," Matt said. "It spoke to me. Right to me. It's *evil,* plain and simple. And the ones that killed Mrs. Petrie...."

"I have no idea what you're talking about. But nothing spoke to you, just as I'm not speaking to you," Gerry smiled. "This is in *your* head. Like it is in everyone's heads. When around this thing, your mind creates what it wants to. Like... Like when someone is on drugs and sees stuff. The stuff isn't there. Their mind conjures it up. It won't do anything if you see something, and you aren't afraid. But if you are afraid... Then again, as I said, I don't know squat. This is you guessing and me, as a memory in here, speaking it aloud. As E said to you, you'll never know for sure. He definitely did, though."

"You're a bad trip then."

"Maybe, yeah."

"Then why are you justifying this thing's existence? I know I wouldn't do that," Matt said, still gripping his gun tight, ready to use if necessary. "How do I know you're not this *thing* trying to save its own ass?"

"Oh, it can eat a bag of dicks and burn to the ground for what it did to me, but don't lie to yourself." He leaned closer. "It's not a person. Or a demon. It's just a parasite."

Matt shook his head. "So all of this, you, here, what? What's the point? Do I only talk to you and wait to die?"

"You can," Gerry said. "But I know I can prove to you I'm not *just* in your head. I have some thoughts that are not yours and never were." He paused and smiled. "Do you wanna see it? The thing that did all this to us? I know where it is, and you don't."

Gerry pointed up behind Matt. "It's right there on the wall," he said. "Let me tell you when I felt *that* in the dark? Well, I screamed until my breath gave out. I think I actually crapped my pants at that point."

Matt's eyes widened as he turned around and pointed the flashlight at the wall behind him.

Embedded in the flesh of the wooden wall, high up, a large, gray, and slimy creature made of tentacles and multiple eyes stared back at him blankly. From within its tentacles, thousands of vines spread out over the walls.

This thing looked like it came from the deepest seas in a distant universe. An ancient creature whose very existence instilled terror in the few unfortunate enough to see it.

"One thing from the very little I know," Gerry said, kindly smiling at the creature, "is it didn't invade us or force its way here. It's part of here."

"Part of here? Part of what?"

"Not what, *who*."

Matt closed his eyes and rubbed his head with the hand carrying the gun. "This is a fever dream. None of this is real."

"It might not be," Gerry shrugged with a laugh. "I've no idea. I know I was dead, but now? I dunno. I'm talking to you. It feels real, right? Am I a ghost now?"

With a mounting frustration, Matt got to his feet, stood back, then stared at the thing on the wall, pointing his flashlight across its many eyes.

After a pause, he raised his weapon at the creature. "I'm done with this," he said with a grimace.

"You don't wanna do that," Gerry said with some fear.

But Matt didn't listen.

He aimed straight at the creature in the wall and fired his gun.

As the bullet hit, it sank deep into the creature's gray body and disappeared without leaving a mark on its slimy skin.

The room instantly shook violently as a whining clacking sounded like a siren. It deafened Matt from every direction. Vines shot out from around the creature, impaling Matt through the arms and legs. His flashlight and gun dropped out of his hand as the collision launched him off his feet. The vines then hurled him out of the beam of his flashlight and deep into the darkness of the back of the room. He slammed hard against the far wall, the vines now through his body, affixing him to the fleshy wood like a pin through the paper on a notice board.

Matt could only scream in the dark. A scream only one person heard.

Through his tear-filled eyes, he grimaced in pain as he stared at where Gerry had just been. Now, though, there was nothing there. Nothing except where the flashlight highlighted the monster in the wall.

It stared back at him with its multitude of eyes as blankly as before.

Matt could not see anything outside of the flashlight's beam. He could not see that against the wall, below where he had been pinned by the vines, someone was cowering in a fetal position, whimpering softly to themselves. Pip. Not a ghost, an apparition, a tree creature, but the real fragile and now slowly dying boy. Terrified, starving, bleeding, and in more pain than anyone should be able to handle.

HAMISH WAS deep inside Cromwell Woods when he woke up from his dreamlike journey from the hospital. As he stood still, his bare feet touching the dirt ground, he felt the immense cold hit him like a sledgehammer.

The darkness of the forest he found himself in was terrifying. Though the moon broke through the treetops, it did little except cast long black shadows in every direction.

No escape was visible to him. There was no north, no

south, no east or west. There were only identical-looking trees in each direction. He truly was lost, with no watch to tell the time and no familiarity with his surroundings. Lost in the trees, lost in time, lost in meaning.

He had ventured into the woods around Hemlock Creek more than he could remember. He knew them well, as did all his friends. But this could have been any forest in any part of the world.

His teeth clattered from shivering, and his tiny body trembled. He would have burst into tears if he had been slightly warmer. But it was too cold to do much of anything now. His body could only tremble and feel a profound numbness.

He had to walk.

He knew he could not wait around here.

He knew how wrong all of this was. How strange it was that he walked there in a daze.

Turning around, he hurriedly walked back from the way he thought he might have come. Any direction was better than none.

With the uneven ground littered with sticks and stones, each step was uncomfortable to take on his soft, exposed soles, especially the one with the bleeding gash.

Each step he took, he waded through the menacing mist covering the ground around him.

He gritted his teeth as hard as he could to stop their chattering, but it was a useless endeavor. He was too cold to have much control. Too distracted by his need to escape.

As he walked, from the corners of his eyes, his mind seemed to play tricks as each shadow he saw looked like a person watching. But he dared not look their way. He had to stay focused, and he had to get home.

Between the trees in front of him, the darkness seemed to thicken as the shadows built into a silhouette as he got nearer. A tall, imposing figure. One he had not seen there before.

Slowing to a halt, Hamish could not look away. Unlike the shadows in his periphery, he stared at this thing head-on unable to avert his gaze. He felt as if his very life depended on it.

Crouching down, his hand blindly scrambled for some protection as he kept staring ahead.

The silhouette in front of him did not move. It simply stood there in his path.

Hamish's hand found a rock, and as he stood up, he hurled it, full force toward the silhouette.

With an echoed wooden thud, the silhouette didn't move. It just stayed there as the rock landed on the soft earth.

Summoning his bravery, Hamish knelt and picked up another rock by his feet.

With it held ready to hurl again, he stepped closer toward the silhouette.

Then again.

Each step was slow and careful.

When he was about two yards away, he hurled the rock forward with all his might.

Clacking off the silhouette loudly, this rock bounced and landed on the dirt.

Confused, Hamish stepped closer until the moonlight's dull glow illuminated what was actually there. It was not a cloaked person or a monster. It was a large entwining of wooden branches, like a sculpture in the shape of a person.

What was it? Was it only a tree he let his imagination transform into a beast?

Shaking his head, he smiled, slightly relieved at it being only a plant, and stepped past it.

Allowing himself to look either side, he saw the other silhouettes he had ignored. They must be the same as this, he rationalized.

He then shook his head, amused at his fear, forgetting the painful cold and his situation for a brief spell.

Turning back to glance at the strange tree sculpture behind him, his blood instantly ran cold.

It was gone.

Nowhere to be seen.

Turning back to run, he skidded to a halt and let out a terrifying scream as the collection of branches in the shape of a person now stood in his path again.

As he clambered to run in another direction, he screamed a third time as another one of these things appeared in his way.

Yet again, he changed direction, his screams now joined with tears, but he slammed straight into a figure. Not a collection of branches but a familiar yet ghostly face.

The corrupted version of his friend, Pip.

"Hello, Hamish," this creature said with a sick grin. "We've been waiting for you for a long time."

The sound of clattering vines filled the woodland, eclipsing Hamish's screams.

Above him, one of the last things he saw before he collapsed was a face. High up, looking down at him. A grinning face in the trees.

FAREWELL

As the morning sun shone through the kitchen window, Emmie walked down the stairs of her house, looking as if she hadn't slept for a week. Her bloodshot eyes watched as her father stood at the kitchen window, his back to her, drinking his morning coffee before he left the house.

Looking at him silently for a moment, she rued that they barely talked anymore. Not like they used to. Since her mother passed, they rarely saw each other, let alone had time to speak. She knew he had been avoiding her for a while to protect himself, as his grief was insurmountable for him to handle. Still, she needed him to know it was all okay, especially after what she planned to do today.

She walked up and hugged her father from behind.

"I love you, dad," she said unsolicited.

As if igniting an engine, Heath Hanson put the coffee cup on a nearby counter, turned, and hugged his daughter as if he had been waiting for permission to do so all this time. "Love you too, scamp." The look on his face was relief, as much as surprise. "You okay? You are, right?"

Emmie closed her eyes as she held on tightly. "Can you come home early tonight? Can we watch a film like we did with mom?"

Heath felt a stirring of emotion. An emotion he had been ignoring for a long time. "Of course, we can," he said, unable to stop a joyful quiver in his voice. "It's a date."

After this simple interaction, Emmie felt a warm glow inside as she walked toward Findley's house across town. If today went as bad as it could, at least her father knew how she felt and nothing was left unsaid.

James and Findley did not ponder anything concerning their families. Both had just met as soon as possible and ransacked their parents' garages for weapons, protection, and anything available. They avoided any contact with their parents by saying they were working on a school project, enough to permit them to do almost anything.

Binh and Kathy Tran were happy James was no longer shutting himself in the room, whereas Amber Scott could only hope her Findley would stay out of trouble. Her efforts thus far had done nothing to stop her son from doing what he wanted, when he wanted. So she chose to stand back and be there when he needed her. She only hoped he would come home at the end of each day.

EMMIE SAW her friends waiting for her on the grass verge in front of the large sign to Fragrant Pines. James and Findley stood below the cursive writing that stated, 'You'll never want to leave.'

Findley picked up the rucksack at his feet, then waved to Emmie.

"We not going to yours anymore?" Emmie asked, confused as she got nearer to them.

"I can't get hold of Pip's mom," James said, shaking his head, "so we're going there now."

"Find anything else in the book?" Findley asked.

Emmie smiled and nodded. "I *think* so. But it depends."

"On?" James asked.

"On whether you can remember something from when you saw Pip."

James looked unsure at Emmie, then Findley. "I told you everything."

"You remember any fog? The Sheriff wrote that there was yellow misty fog every time the thing appeared to him."

"Are mist and fog the same thing?" Findley asked.

James' expression dropped as his mouth hung open. "Oh damn!" He clicked his fingers repeatedly as he remembered. "There was yellow smoke everywhere. I forgot!"

"Wait... Is smoke the same as mist and fog as well?" Findley reframed his question.

"I *think* the mist's part of it," Emmie replied to James, ignoring Findley. "I don't know what it is, but I think it means when we're in danger. That's what the book says. Every time the sheriff saw stuff, the mist was there. Every time. So if we see it—"

"We run like cluck," Findley said, beaming.

"How d'you not swear all the time by accident?" Emmie asked, caught off-guard for a moment.

"Talent, dear Emmie, talent," Findley replied. "And years of getting grounded for swearing."

"It sure is something; talent's a stretch, though," Emmie said. "Now, what's the plan?"

"I figured it out," James said, clicking his fingers. Smiling, he reached into the bag on Findley's shoulder. "You know the book said fire won't work?" he continued, bringing out a large water pistol.

Emmie nodded.

"My folks bought this stuff when we moved in. Kills plants dead."

"That sheriff was thinking too old school. Fire? Nah!"

Findley said as he shook his head. "Chemicals! That's what we gotta use. And this stuff he found, damn, it's strong."

James put the water pistol back into the bag with a victorious expression.

"Is it safe for *us*?" Emmie asked with concern.

Findley spun the open bag off his shoulder, reached in, and produced a decorator filter mask. "Got three of these to protect us. Three water pistols, three masks. Box said they protect from dust and toxic stuff, which should do it. My mom bought 'em when she was gonna redecorate, but never did. Now they're all ours." Putting the mask back in, he peered into his bag. "Also got some hand saws, cos, you know, wood hates saws. A knife—"

Emmie's smile faltered. "We can't really be doing this, can we?"

Findley looked at her, then at James, as the reality of the situation set in.

They all were out of their depths but were putting on as brave faces as they could muster.

They all knew this was dangerous—*Too* dangerous in fact, and also *very* stupid of them to consider. But none of that mattered now. It was not about safety.

"If we don't do it," Findley said. "Who will? The police'll try, but they're not lookin' in the right places. Sarah was gonna go to the woods with the Sheriff last night, but we can't find her."

"For Pip then," James said boldly as he fought the urge to run home. "Besides, it's daytime, and the first sign of any creepy stuff, we are running the hell away."

"Okay," Emmie agreed. "For Pip."

"I wish Hamish was here," Findley added.

"I called his house," Emmie said. "His dads must be at the hospital still. Guess it's safer than with us."

They turned and began their journey to Sarah's house.

"Find the house, get Pip, get out. Simple," Findley said with a laugh as he put an arm around both of his friends. "Hamish is gonna be so annoyed he missed out."

"She went to look for Pip," the Reverend said morosely. "I told her not to, the police told us to let them do their job, but she said the Sheriff's gone missing... I don't know what to do."

Findley, James, and Emmie looked up at Pip's father, unsure how to respond.

"Do you know where?" Emmie asked after a few moments.

The Reverend shook his head. "Sorry," he said as he closed the door on them, not wanting to engage with them anymore.

They remained looking up at the sizable wooden door for a moment.

"The Sheriff's gone missing?" James said under his breath nervously.

Findley paced the porch, then said, "I bet he's in the woods looking for Pip."

"You think she's with him?" Emmie asked.

"Hope so." Findley turned to James, "Think I'm gonna let you go into the woods first, okay? Em, and I'll hang back."

"What?" James asked with genuine surprise.

"Cos you know all those kung fu chop-socky moves, right," Findley said with a smile.

James shook his head and rolled his eyes. "Dude, I'm from Vietnam!" he said.

Findley's face dropped. "No! I didn't mean that. You took that karate class, remember? I was talking about that, not... not... I didn't—" He stopped in his tracks as he saw James holding back a laugh. "Oh, you *asshole*!"

"You swore!" Emmie exclaimed. "Finally!"

The laugh was the last these three would share.

HEMLOCK CREEK HAD AWAKENED to confusion.

The Sheriff was nowhere to be found.

The care home, the last place he was known to have gone, was now a suspected crime scene. But he was not the only one missing. Doctor Turner had not gone home that night.

The caregiver who visited Mike Fisk in the morning had reported that the house at the end of Lamplight Crescent was empty and there was a large hole in the wall near where Mad Mike usually sat.

The old Edson Dam had seemingly disappeared under more forest that had appeared almost overnight. Each new tree looked like it had always been there, not only for one day.

But most worrying to the town was the disappearance of Hamish Flynn. The CCTV recorded him walking out of his hospital room and out into the night wearing nothing but his gown.

With their lack of leadership, the Sheriff's department didn't know where to start or what to do. They had called in for help from the next county, but all they could do in the meantime was wait.

Little did they know from the center of Cromwell Woods and out onto every street, a fine mist, barely noticeable in the daytime, slithered its way down each asphalt street—a horrible precursor of things to come.

SHERIFF MATT BENSON was not awake.

From his unconscious state, he had little grasp on where he was nor any memory of what had just happened to him.

Instead of the usual dreams, his mind was awash with something else. Something had invaded his thoughts.

He had no recollection of the vines that now impaled his body and held him against the soft, meaty, and wet wooden wall. He did not know that, at that very moment, the vines that had pierced him were also secreting a thick golden substance into his blood supply and his dreams.

The images he saw in his mind were colored in the same hue of gold as the substance currently invading him, as if it were a dye and coloring everything in its path. Along with the color, came something else. A permeating thought. One that was not his. One that was all-consuming.

In his dreams, Matt was not Matt. He was a bigger and better version of himself, with a more chiseled jaw and a trimmer, muscular physique. This 'dream Matt' was a teenager again, sitting in a café talking to Sarah Charles. Not Sarah Kaminsky—for here, she was the same as she used to be. Young and in love with him. Staring at him like he was the only one on earth.

"I'm hungry," she said with a coy smile as she picked up the menu and looked over it.

With a chuckle, Matt, too, looked down at the menu in

his hands, but as he read, his expression turned to confusion as he saw the items listed.

Blood.

Muscle.

Brain.

Eyes.

Hands.

Spine.

Bowels.

Liver.

Hair.

"What is this?" he muttered.

"I'm hungry," Sarah reiterated.

A waiter sidled up. "May I take your order?" he asked.

Recognizing the voice, Matt looked up from the disturbing menu and was met with the glare of Mike Fisk. Not the Mikey of his youth, but the legless gross man he had become, sat in his moldy chair right in the middle of the walkway next to their table. Somehow he was high enough to loom over them both.

Sarah turned to meet Mike's gaze. "I'm hungry," she said again, almost petulant this time.

"*We are* hungry," Mike said with a sneer as if it were a competition. "Hungry, hungry, *hungry*," he said louder at her with each successive word.

Sarah then began to cry. "But I'm hungry," she blubbed.

"Sarah?" Matt said, reaching a hand across the table to her.

"*We* are so hungry," she sobbed.

Mike then turned back to his menu. It had all changed.

Matt's Blood.

Matt's Muscle.

Matt's Brain.

Matt's Eyes.

Matt's Hands.

Matt's Spine.

Matt's Bowels.

Matt's Liver.

Matt's Hair.

"*We are so hungry*," Mike and Sarah said in unison as they turned their gazes toward him.

Then crawling over the table, Sarah's expression looked pained. "So hungry, so very hungry," she said. But as she spoke, a small vine protruded from within her mouth.

Looking up at Mike, Matt shrieked as some vines curled their way out of his mouth as they did with Sarah's and broke through his eyeballs from within, exploding their jelly over his cheeks and down his beard. Mike did not react in pain, though. He just kept repeating, "Hungry, hungry, *hungry*...."

"*Hungry*..."

On any typical night when Matt was having a nightmare, he would have woken up at this point in a cold sweat. But now, in this twisted golden dreamscape, he was not about to be given that particular gift.

He felt every tooth that dug into his skin, every fingernail that clawed at him, every nerve that was shredded in pain. He felt his whole body being slowly ripped apart and consumed, way beyond the point of death.

"She's in the woods then," Findley said, as the three of them passed Sarah's car. It had been parked up on the side of the road by Cromwell Woods. "Guess she went in with the Sheriff after all."

"How does this place look worse than yesterday?" James asked, looking at the dead trees around them.

Emmie looked up. "It's bigger, right?" She glanced down the road on either side of them. "Trees never came up to the roadside... did they? Wasn't there a path?"

"Pip's mom's got the map, hasn't she?" James said with some annoyance. "She should have told us what she was doin'."

"It's Pip," Emmie said. "I get it." She then looked at where the grass verge used to be. Now it was just dead earth. Even the asphalt nearest the tree line looked grayer, more aged.

"This is stupid. This is so heckin' stupid." Findley shook his head. "We shouldn't be here."

At that moment, Emmie noticed the thin, barely visible mist drifting an inch above the asphalt.

"The masks!" she said urgently. "Fin, get the masks and guns!"

Before anyone could think, a scream rang out faintly in the distance.

"What the hell was that?" James said.

Emmie and Findley looked confused.

"Helllllllp meeeeeeee!" the voice echoed louder from deep within the Cromwell woods.

James' eyes went wider all of a sudden.

He knew that voice.

"Pip!" he screamed as he sprinted, without thinking, ahead through the tree line and into the woods.

"James, no!" Emmie shouted after him, but he was gone.

Before Findley could run after James, Emmie grabbed him by the arm. "Masks! Now!" she demanded.

"What?" Findley asked in a panic. "Really?"

"It's getting bigger," she shouted urgently. "The mist is *here!* Look at your feet! The trees are *growing!* Get the damn guns out, now!"

He didn't need any more convincing.

It was only a few seconds until they were both off, water pistols in hand, masks on, in the direction James had run.

"James!" Emmie called out, "Come back!"

They could not see him, but they heard his shouts.

"Pip! Where are you?" James called out from deeper in the woodland.

"What did he hear?" Findley asked Emmie as they hurriedly moved through the woods in the direction of James's voice. "You hear anythin'?"

"Not a damn thing!" she replied.

"Pip! Where are you?!" James shouted and ran as fast as he could through the trees, but the cries he had heard from Pip had since stopped.

Coming to a clearing, James slowed his pace and looked around. "Pip?!" he shouted.

Nothing.

There was no sound here at all. Not even the wind in the trees. It was almost like being inside a vacuum; the lack of sound was oppressive.

He breathed deeply. Not knowing the yellow mist was being carried in the air and filling his lungs.

A panic quickly sank in as James realized what he had

done. His instinct had sent him blindly running to save his friend without a second thought for his own safety.

"Guys?" James called out. "Emmie? Fin?" His shouts grew more desperate.

He then noticed the mist at his feet, getting thicker and more golden by the second, but it was too late. He was without a mask. Without protection.

Emmie ran just ahead of Findley.

Faster and faster.

In a panic.

Faster.

Faster.

Suddenly, her foot caught the underside of an exposed root, breaking her ankle with a loud snap.

She screamed as her body was thrown down to the side, between two trees, and down a steep incline over a high dirt ridge. Through thorny bushes, she tumbled round and around. The pain in her foot was blinding, and the bone was exposed through her sock. Blood spilled outward with ease. She had lost her grip on the water pistol as she fell, as well as the foldable saw she had tucked into her belt.

Her spin down into the dark shadows continued until it ended abruptly, with her back colliding with a large tree trunk, stopping her in her tracks with a painful crack. She yelped like a wounded animal as her ribs snapped outward in her chest, lacerating her lungs.

"Emmie!" screamed Findley from the top of the ridge.

Wincing as the pain shot up her spine and through her body, Emmie tried to move, but instantly, everything had changed. All the pain, all the feeling, even the coldness she had ignored until now, disappeared. Every bit of sensation she had now seeped away as a new terrifying numbness crept in and consumed her.

As she tried to scream out for help, she faltered. With her lungs collapsing from the impact, her breathing was desperate, weak, wheezing, and unable to grab hold of any sound.

She lay, contorted at the base of a tree, face down in the dirt, hoping for a miracle, but instead, she only saw the mist crawling around her, slipping over her. Reaching inside her lungs as she gasped. It was only now she realized her mask had also slipped off, and she was left helpless against whatever was to come at her.

"Emmie!"

She heard Findley's desperate cries to her but couldn't reply.

Looking down the ridge, Findley could only see the shadows and the yellow mist. The sun did not reach down to where his friend had fallen.

Holding his water pistol, he glanced around, knowing the mist signaled only one thing.

FROM OUT OF the shadows down where Emmie lay, something emerged.

Emmie did not hear the moving branches nor know what was crouching down beside her.

She would have been terrified on any ordinary occasion, but her vision dimmed as her breathing weakened. She could see, but she could not react.

From out of the bushes, on tendrils of thick vines, a ghostly doppelgänger of Sarah bent down and peered into

Emmie's failing eyes. With a terrifyingly large grin, Sarah was bursting with flittering vines from within her body.

A look of curiosity crossed its familiar yet haunting face as the vines retreated from her mouth, and the smile shrank to a frown. Extending her gray hand, this phantom Sarah touched Emmie's face. Prodding it lightly.

And after that, Emmie's world went dark.

After her short life, Emmaleen Hanson left the mortal coil not from a supernatural cause, as so many had in this town, but from a simple accident. Tragic as it was, Emmie had felt no fear. As the numbness took hold of her, she instinctively knew it was her life's closing chapter. Her last thought was not remorse for her loss, nor terror at the monster now looking in her eyes, but happiness that she had told her father that she loved him.

Findley screamed as he got to the base of the gully that Emmie had fallen into and saw the vast collection of vines now piercing her deceased body—lifting her and pulling her apart bit by bit—limb by limb.

He did not see the doppelgänger of Sarah. He saw no human attributes. The mask had kept the visions away, and what he saw was what was real. What was actual.

Alerted by the intrusion, the monstrous vines turned to face Findley.

He could not tell what scared him the most, the sight of his friend's body mutilated or the supernatural beast coming after him.

He screamed again as the vines advanced rapidly in his direction. The mask he wore did nothing to lessen the volume of sound.

Without a pause, he raised the water pistol and fired a jet of chemicals at the monster.

The monster squealed a horrific cry of pain as the liquid collided with the vines and retreated. Its vines smoked as the chemical acid burned into it on impact.

Jet after jet, Findley fired at the beast as it backed away. Both of them screamed—the beast from pain, Findley from fury.

Within seconds, the vines had disappeared back into the dark.

Panicked, Findley turned back to where Emmie was, but nothing was left of her. The ground was covered in blood, and tiny blobs of unidentifiable flesh were amongst the undergrowth. Not even those bits could be seen in this dark, and through the mist.

Findley couldn't stop the tears as he sprinted back up to the ridge, terrified and distraught.

JAMES WALKED through the woods in a daze. Despite it being morning, the sun abandoned the area. There, it seemed like a winter's evening, with a freeze setting in as little light shone through the thick dead branches above, making the yellow mist more visible and more surreal.

He could see the shadows around him. Looking like people were watching—but he shut those thoughts out. But even while forcing this idea away, it didn't stop the primal fear from ripping through his mind without mercy.

He walked at speed quickly away from the shadows. Convincing himself that he was being stupid. That it was all a lie. That these were just woods.

"James?" came Sarah's familiar voice from far ahead of him. "Is that you?" she called out.

Stopping in his tracks, James gasped.

"James?" the voice called again. "It's Pip's mom... I'm stuck! I can't reach the branches. Can you help? Please!"

The shadows between the trees didn't move, but he still glanced around, half expecting monsters to come rushing out of them. But they were shadows and nothing more. His mind was playing tricks on him.

"Pleaaaase," Sarah said again, sounding very much in pain.

James gritted his teeth. *I have to stop being afraid*, he tried to convince himself.

"I'm coming," he shouted as he hurried forward, racing toward the large dead brush of thick branches ahead.

"Please, James," she shouted again, the sound of sobs following.

James raced around the brush, climbing over a fallen tree, where he expected to find Sarah. And find her he did.

With long spiked branches rising like dozens of antlers, Sarah's corpse was skewered amongst them. No part of her body was left intact, no part aside from her face. The face that stared outward toward him. Her mouth hung open wide in a perma-scream. Locked in death in its last expression.

"James, please," the voice of Sarah said, but the actual dead body just remained motionless.

James couldn't scream. Couldn't do anything except walk backward in shock. Walk away from this grotesque tableau.

"Why aren't you helping, James? Why?"

This dislocated voice was haunting as the dead body's milky eyes stared out.

He forgot about the shadows in the tree line all around him.

Forgot until his back hit something solid.

Screaming, he spun around, but his mouth was immediately covered by someone's hand.

Findley.

Still wearing his mask and carrying a water pistol, he grabbed James.

"Shhhh," Findley said, panicked.

James immediately threw his arms around his friend with relief and fear.

Findley then saw what had happened to Sarah.

He closed his eyes briefly but pushed away every bit of fear. He needed to get him and James out of this forest.

"Where's Emmie?" James asked.

But before Findley could answer, they turned around and saw the huge looming house made of dead trees and creeping, moving vines. Sat right in their way. Impossibly in the place where they had come from. It had appeared entirely without a sound, as if summoned by magic.

In its malformed doorway, stood Pip, smiling—the ghostly Pip. At least, that is what James saw. Findley could only see a collection of moving, undulating vines.

"Welcome, friends," the thing said with a horrible smile. "I am afraid I cannot let you in. We are too close to our birth. We cannot risk not being."

Findley, though, could only hear the clattering of vines.

"Give us the real Pip!" James screamed, still holding onto Findley

Findley meanwhile looked at his friend with curiosity, then at the house, as everything fell into place.

He understood it all in this one moment.

He looked around the thick yellow mist, then back at the house.

"I know you're not him," James screamed at the ghostly Pip again.

He also remembered in the journal, all those that survived, none of them had worn a mask.

Even as he thought this may be the stupidest thing he would ever do, Findley lifted the mask from his face and dropped it to the floor.

"What do we do?" James asked, still gripping Findley.

Findley took in a deep series of breaths.

It only took a few moments for the vines in the doorway to change, to become the same thing as what James saw. The horrific Pip. Smiling hungrily at them.

"It will be quick," this Pip said. "But it *will* be painful."

Findley calmly removed his backpack, reached in, pulled out the spare water pistol, then handed it to James.

"You ready, buddy?" Findley whispered with a nervous smile, lifting his weapon.

James nodded, unsure, but held onto the water pistol for dear life.

At the doorway, the ghostly Pip began to look concerned.

OUROBOROS

Within its dark and flesh-like walls, Pip had no idea of the time or space he was in. He just felt the pain. The terrible, terrible pain. Above him, still impaled to the wall, Sheriff Matt Benson hung with vines piercing his legs and arms. The vines drooped loosely from his body and onto the floor, trailing their way back up to the opposite side of the room where the creature lay embedded, watching them both—watching everything.

The small flashlight still shone its narrow beam over a part of this creature, illuminating the dark shark-like eyes that adorned its gray, moist body.

Matt was coming to from his terrible elongated nightmare. The bleeding from the vines stabbing through various parts of his body had slowed to a trickle. He could not move, though. Even the slightest twitch caused him to scream in pain, a scream he had little energy to make now. Through his bleary eyes, as they half opened, reality was cast into question as he caught sight of the surreal, semi-lit creature on the other side of the terrifying, deathly room.

Suddenly a deep and booming slurping sound could be heard throughout each wall around him.

Matt strained to focus and tried to discern what was making the noise. He could see that the creature seemed to tremble with each slurping sound, as if what was making the noise was in contact with it, making its strange body shake with intense vibrations. He *remembered* that noise, though. He had heard it just as he lost consciousness before he found himself in this undulating room filled with monsters and bones.

But this time, after the noise ceased, Gerry had not appeared like before. Even though Matt chalked up his appearance to some kind of fever dream, he had hoped to have seen his dead friend again, hoping the noise was the precursor to his arrival.

The slurping noise then resumed.

As it got louder and closer, the sound of wood cracking soon combined with it.

Matt was in no state to be able to shield his ears from the cacophony of cracks and strange eating sounds that built up deafeningly around him.

There was movement from the middle of the darkened ceiling, far from the grace of the flashlight's illumination. As the wood moved and pulsed ferociously, it soon began to part. A small aperture within it began to open to a large circular hole. From within this gap, thick golden liquid dripped to the floor below. Dropping down where it landed in a thick, viscous pool. As this expanding fissure grew, something then came down from within it.

A body. The sound of it landing on the floor with a wet thud brought Matt slightly out of his daze.

The hole in the ceiling, having dropped its contents into the room, began to recede and close itself up until it was as it was before. The slurping sound stopped and was soon nothing but a remembered echo.

All the while, the beast was still in the wall, still in the wall watching the deposited object that lay prostrate on the floor.

Though mostly hidden in darkness, Matt saw a leg lying in the flashlight's beam. A bare, pale leg.

"H-hello," Matt managed to say with weakness and strain. "Are you okay?" After he spoke, he realized that the body might not even be living. It may not even be whole. It may be the remnants of a massacre. Who knows in—

A groan.

It cut into Matt's thoughts as the leg he saw in the half-light moved.

"Hello?" he asked again, trying to grasp every shred of strength left in his body.

"I—" came a weak word from the darkness, "I can't see." The voice trembled. "Why can't I see?"

As the body moved, more of it came into the flashlight's beam.

Hamish.

His body was lacerated and bleeding through his ripped hospital gown. His face, too, as a long bloody wound ran across his forehead, sending blood down and into his eyes.

"Hamish?" Matt said as he recognized the boy.

"W-who is that?" Hamish asked, terrified.

"The Sheriff. Sheriff Benson"

Hamish smiled with some relief at the familiarity he had found. His palms wiping his eyes made little difference to his sight. It was not the blood on his face, but he also felt the golden liquid in his eyes, causing them to shut without command out of self-preservation. Like a thick honey, it seemed to be now crystallizing. He clawed at the substance, trying to pull and rub it off him.

"I need your help, Hamish," Matt said as he tried to sound stronger than he felt.

Hamish's efforts allowed his eyes to partly open as he managed to rub a large portion of the gelatinous liquid away. But when he did manage to open them, they stung him horribly.

He grimaced loudly as the pain hit.

Matt wanted to help him, but there was simply nothing he could do.

Again, Hamish attempted to open his eyes fully, and the pain returned. He could see little in the dark room anyway. He tried again, this time looking the other way, and he caught sight of the flashlight on the floor near him.

In a panic, he scrambled over to that light and grabbed hold of it.

"Over here," Matt said, his voice strained as Hamish picked up the light.

Alerted by his voice, Hamish turned the flashlight in Matt's direction. Though he could not see for long, he kept opening his eyelids for a few painful seconds, trying to make his way across the room as quickly as possible.

"Where am I?" Hamish asked as he stepped uncertainly across the meaty, moving floor. He tried to focus, but everything he tried to see remained blurry.

"I wish I knew," Matt replied. "I need you to help me get down."

As Hamish got nearer, the sight of Matt came into his limited view. Raised a couple of feet off the ground, he saw, blearily, the Sheriff attached to the wall, with the vines pierced through his arms, shoulders, and thighs.

"Please, Hamish, you gotta help me down from here," Matt pleaded.

Before Hamish could answer, he noticed something below Matt, something trembling and bloodied. Turning the flashlight onto it, Hamish could *just* make out a face. A face contorted in agony on a weak body that could barely move.

"Pip!" Hamish exclaimed, almost unbelieving, as he tried to see clearer, keeping his eyes open that much longer to see his friend. But each time he tried, the pain of the burning liquid in his eyes grew more intense.

Pip did not reply. He just lay in a fetal position, shaking in a bloody mess. Hamish could make out in the flashlight's beam that chunks of flesh were missing from all over his friend's body.

"What?" Matt's eyes widened as he had not even seen what was crumpled below him.

Hamish hurried over to his friend, trying to keep his eyes open as he shone the light downward. But Pip was not responsive. He only groaned weakly, gripping his life by a thread.

"Oh God, oh God," Hamish said in a panic. "C'mon, Pip."

"Get me down!" The Sheriff said with a painful authority. "Quick!"

Like an electric shock, the command from the impaled policeman made Hamish jump back and look up at him.

"You gotta grab those creeper things coming out of me," Matt said. "Pull 'em as hard as you can. I need you to pull one from my arm. I'll do the rest."

Hamish tried to focus, but his eyes still screamed at him in stinging pain.

"Hurry," Matt added. "Please, Hamish, please."

Trying his best to focus on the vines coming from the Sheriff, Hamish rubbed his eyes again, trying anything to see more and without the agony. He moved the flashlight across the vines on the floor as he tried to tell which one to pick up.

"The one next to your foot," Matt said, having already seen which vine he needed help with. "Grab it, and no matter what, keep yanking at it until it comes away. Even if I'm screaming, you understand me?"

Hamish understood little about what was happening. He remembered the oversized silhouettes that attacked him in the woods, cutting him with their branches. Dragging him to that house. Forcing him through the giant mouth-like hole in the floor. All while the terrifying versions of Pip, Adam, and Mrs. Petrie looked on—then the blackness. For so long, it was only the blackness. All until he fell through the ceiling of this room. He was running on zero energy, hoping that it would all end soon if he kept moving. He would get home or even wake up from this nightmare.

Grabbing the vine, Hamish squeezed his eyes closed and pulled it with all his might.

Matt felt vibrations in the wound on his arm as the vine was being yanked. Searing into him, the agony made him scream through his gritted teeth.

Hamish made a quiet yelp as he froze, realizing that he had caused the Sheriff's pain.

Matt grimaced, raising his voice with urgency. "Pull!"

On command, Hamish yanked at the vine again. It did not come any looser.

"Pull!" Matt screamed again in increasing agony.

With his eyes still closed, Hamish dropped the flashlight to the floor to better grip the vine and yanked it back as hard as possible.

The sound of cracking filled the void as the vine was

pulled out from the wall, from Matt's forearm, and into the room like a loose rope.

With a yell, Matt didn't let the almost debilitating torment slow him. Now with one, yet injured, arm free, he grabbed another vine that stuck out of his shoulder and pulled at it hard.

It came free from the wall with some ease, but as it did, the weight of his body proved too much for the rest of the vines.

He fell to the floor as the remaining vines snapped with weakness.

But these were not typical vines. They were not silent pieces of growing wood. These were an extension of the creature.

As they snapped, the room shook, and the creature violently trembled in the darkness.

The loose vines reared up, and as they did, Matt looked up from the floor and grabbed the flashlight. Turning it back into the room, he saw them up and ready to attack them.

Hamish's eyes widened at the horror.

FINDLEY SCREAMED.

Not in pain.

Not in sadness.

In anger.

Standing shoulder to shoulder with James in the wooden house, they fired jets of acidic chemicals at all approaching things.

The ghostly Pip was at the far side of this open room, quivering as the acid covered it. Its body was breaking apart and showing its viny insides pulsing almost like a heartbeat.

Above them, an angry, contorted face could be seen amongst the tree branches.

James felt bravery and a purpose, unlike anything he had ever felt. He just felt righteous. As he fired the water pistol at the large branches that threatened to attack them, as they smoked and dissolved around him, he did not notice the stinging in his now bloodshot eyes from the chemicals.

As they stood on one side of the room, back the creature's vines with chemicals, Findley kept one eye on the floor. The floor looked like a sizable vine-filled mouth.

As soon as the creature that looked like Pip had dissolved and the vines on the floor began to move, Findley motioned at the mouth-like opening to his friend. "Down there! Aim there!"

As they both fired the caustic liquid downward in unison, the whole house around them reacted violently.

If they had looked up, they would have seen the branches that made up the 'tree man' separate and the image of the angry face disappear.

As the chemicals hit the flesh-like wood, the floor mouth began to open and close, exposing a deep passage beneath.

MATT STOOD PROTECTIVELY in front of Hamish, holding the flashlight up to the oncoming danger, ignoring his wounds that were seeping blood, and taking his strength away bit by bit.

The vines were ready to strike.

Hamish closed his eyes, not from the pain but from the fear of what would come.

At that moment, before the vines could strike, the aperture in the ceiling rumbled. Then the whole room rumbled.

The vines turned around like snakes looking around themselves.

Then all hell broke loose.

The hole in the ceiling opened and closed rapidly, its only reaction to the damage caused by Findley and James.

In the darkness at the back of the room, unseen by anyone, the creature's whole body shook, its multitude of eyes closed tightly as it felt the pain the rest of the house did.

A clacking squeal rang out from all the monstrousness.

But over that, as Matt aimed the flashlight around, trying to focus on anything that made sense, a voice could be heard that made both him and Hamish smile.

"Die you, futhermockers!"

That battle cry rang out from far away but close enough to hear over the screams of the beasts.

Hamish smiled, not having to see his friend to know that it was him shouting. "Fin!"

Matt turned and saw the body of Pip curled up and almost expired against the wall. Without thinking, he handed Hamish the flashlight, turned back, and hobbled over to Pip. He bent down and picked him up. The pain that screamed out of his wounds was incredible, but he had no intention of succumbing to any of it.

"Quick!" Matt shouted to Hamish as he nodded to the hole in the ceiling where the shouts of Fin could be heard.

The vines around them stood trembling and not attacking, as if paralyzed with torment.

As they got to the base of the ceiling hole that slightly opened and closed, Matt and Hamish saw glimpses of what was above; through twenty feet of a plant-coated hole, they could see the light. And in the light, James and Fin sprayed their water pistols around the hole.

"Hey!" Hamish cried out. Though still in pain and blurry, his eyes saw enough to send him waves of joy and relief.

"What?" Fin looked down, confused, as he saw his friend smiling back. But he could not see the Sheriff or Pip from his vantage point.

"Hamish?" James yelled.

"What the hell you doing down there?" Findley asked.

"We got Pip!" Hamish shouted gleefully.

"We?" Findley replied.

Without engaging with them, Matt moved Pip over his shoulder, reached up into the hole, and grabbed a handful of vines. As he took hold, he grimaced in pain but could also sense the agony the creature now felt as the vines shuddered in his hand like a wounded animal.

Matt turned to Hamish. "Can you climb?"

Unsure if he could, Hamish nodded nonetheless.

BACK ON THE first floor of the house, all was not won. As Hamish and James looked down gleefully, James' happy expression soon dropped as he doubted his own eyes.

"How do we know it's them?" he asked Findley as he saw his friend's happy expression drop.

As they looked at each other worriedly, they overlooked the expanse of vines that now encircled the strange house.

Thousands of wooden tentacles loomed over the house as the monster from Cromwell Woods began to reveal itself.

From the fleshy wooden room deep below them, unbeknownst to Matt or Hamish, who was now busily climbing up the hole with Pip unconscious and flopping over Matt's shoulder, the creature with many eyes was enraged with fury and pain. The branches that grew from within it and spread out of the house and across the whole woodland were now silently being called back to fight. They then began to spin around the house in a frenzy.

Like a protective ink, the yellow mist billowed out from every pore of this attacking monster, from each of its branches, causing a typhoon of vines to turn yellow. Its thickness soon blocked out all the sunlight.

A hurricane of clacking and howls erupted as the tremendous power of the vines outside made themselves known to the house.

Findley and James glanced away from the hole and out of the windows and, in that split second, saw that they had not won the war. Not in the slightest. They had only won their small battle.

Despite the weapons readily in their hands, both had no time to attack as the vines from outside burst through the walls of the house, decimating and absorbing all fleshy wood it touched into their ranks, as the house slowly became part of the aggressive tempest.

The noise grew and grew to immense levels as Findley and James fired their weapons blindly, terrified at the house being decimated around them. But the jets of chemicals from their plastic guns did little against the sheer size of the enemy that spun around them, taking all the walls and ceiling with it until all that was left was this cyclone of vines and yellow gas revolving violently around them. Even if their weapons could have more effect, if they found the correct place to aim, it would be short-lived, as now their liquid ammunition was almost depleted.

From the tiny glimpses of woodland beyond this cyclone, James and Findley could not notice that the woods beyond this violence was changing. Shifting. Morphing. Not just where in the forest they were—as the house was prone to do—but *when*. Seasons changed in an instant. Flitting between summer, fall, winter, and spring in a heartbeat. One moment the trees beyond were dead, then alive, then gone, then saplings. Shift. Shift. Shift.

"Damn!" Findley shouted almost inaudibly as his gun ran dry. He turned to James, unsure of what to do next. But vines sprung up from around them before he could formulate a plan. They collided as they bundled together, entwining into a figure. This figure appeared through the wall of the spinning fury around them. It soon formed into a familiar face.

"Why did you let me die, Findley?" the ghostly form of Emmaleen said with a sad expression.

"No!" James screamed as he realized his friend's final fate. He turned to Findley, "She's alive! She *has* to be alive!"

The tears in Findley's eyes said otherwise.

Emmaleen suddenly grinned as her whole body broke apart, and the vines rejoined the cyclone.

They were too distracted to see Matt climb out of the hole in the floor beside them, a dying Pip in his grasp.

"Help me!" Matt screamed, pulling Findley and James' attention back to him.

Through their upset, both rushed to pull Matt out, grabbing Pip off his back.

"Hey!" Findley screamed, his voice almost a whisper amongst the whirling horror of vines around them. The damage to Pip's body was now apparent. His face and whole body were littered with hundreds of lacerations and chunks of flesh missing. One of his legs had been almost eaten through.

"Where's Hamish?" James asked in a panic, realizing that his friend was not there.

Matt turned back into the hole, which was closing inward, more and more by the second. He saw Hamish climbing halfway up the vines. Slow and pained, but the fastest he could go.

The vines in the hole were no longer dormant but instead flicked at Hamish as he pulled his weight upwards. Each flick sliced the bare skin where they hit.

"Help me!" Hamish cried out.

Matt held his hand into the hole, reaching out to grab him.

As the vines flicked and sliced, Hamish pulled himself up slowly. Each cut on his body sapped his energy bit by bit.

"Grab my hand!" Matt shouted down.

But Hamish felt helpless.

"Grab it!" Matt screamed. "Please!"

The hole was closing in faster around him. The vines were getting more vicious.

"Hamish!" Findley screamed, joining in calling for his friend.

"Reach out!" James added.

Above them, the immense cyclone of vines no longer

stood idly by. It began to close in. Like an ever-decreasing circle, it got smaller and smaller. Its branches were like razors, ready to lacerate anything they collided with.

Matt reached down. He stretched his hand out as far as it would go.

The hole closed in more and more.

The vines around them attacked with whips.

"Now!" Matt shouted in desperation.

With the last of his strength, Hamish let go of the moving vines he clutched, then launched himself off the wall and up to Matt's beckoning grip.

Their palms collided. Matt smiled as he took Hamish's weight, ignoring the pain. But as he was about to pull upward, a collection of vines reached up from below and wrapped around the boy's ankle. Trying to yank him downward.

A terrible fear filled Hamish's eyes as he stared up at Matt, dreading the worst.

Matt cried out in pain as he tried to overcome the increasing force.

"Don't let go!" Hamish screamed.

The vines continued to battle against the Sheriff's grip by pulling the boy down, as above them, the violent storm of wood and thorn closed in.

Then, for a second, time stopped for Sheriff Matthew Benson. As he held Hamish in his grip, he could only think of one thing. One terrible thing started to gnaw at his mind.

Let.

Hamish.

Go.

"Please!" Hamish cried. "Don't let me go!"

Let.

Hamish.

Go.

"Help!" Hamish cried out again as the vines pulled and pulled and pulled at his ankle. Digging into his skin. Pulling so hard it caused his pleas to turn to screams.

Let.

Hamish.

Go.

Matt closed his eyes as he released his grip. Releasing it for reasons he could not fathom. Hamish's eyes widened as he did so, realizing that his would-be savior had done the unthinkable to him.

No words were said as the howling wails of the violent storm of vines closed down on them from above, only a shared glance of sorrow.

As the boy fell into the darkness below, Matt had little time to react as he pulled back, and the hole below him closed.

James screamed as a vine shot out of the cyclone and whipped him across his back with its thorny tip, lacerating him on impact.

Findley moved to help his friend, but more thorned vines shot out at them.

HAMISH HAD FALLEN. Fallen for further than he thought possible. Further than the few yards he had climbed.

Having eventually landed back onto the grotesque, flesh wooden floor of the creature's room, his vision was now nil. The hole had closed above him, and the flashlight he once held was gone.

Pain shot up from his ankle as he tried to get to his feet,

causing him to collapse downward. Immediately reaching, his hands felt wet. Agonizing wetness. His fingers touched a flap of torn skin that burned to his touch. He knew that vines had damaged him, but he could not see the extent, only feel it, and it felt horrific.

The clacking sound approached, as well as a thunderous squelching.

Without thinking, Hamish crawled away from it. Still, instead of making his way across the large room, he immediately hit a wall.

Reaching back, he traced his way along the wall in a panic, moving along to escape the sound that got closer.

But his hand hit another wall.

The sound of moving flesh and cracking wood also got louder and clearer, as if whatever made it was less than a couple of feet away from him, which it was in this darkness.

His mind a whirl, his body almost at the breaking point, Hamish did the only thing he could think of to do.

Gritting his teeth, he reached his hand back and dug his fingers into the soft and flesh-like wooden wall behind him. Gouging at it as if he was frantically digging a hole.

Whatever was in the room with him then made a noise akin to a painful howl, and the tiny room shook thunderously.

This only made Hamish double down and continue at his most frantic pace. With each hand, he grabbed the soft wall and ripped out as large a piece as he could. Digging in and in, he began to scream in urgency and anger.

Rip.

Gouge.

Rip.

Gouge.

Faster.

Faster

Gouge.

Rip.

All the while, the thing in the darkness behind him did not attack. It just screamed its strange and surreal scream.

The room shook more and more until Hamish's entire world spun.

Shifting on its axis, the whole place lost its gravity and spun around as if it had joined the cyclone above, below, or wherever it was.

But this did not stop Hamish, determined to keep digging, clawing, and crawling into the fleshy wall. Scrambling blindly into the darkness, he was fighting for his life.

As he pulled his agonizing ankle along the hole, he kept digging and digging, And the room kept spinning and spinning.

The unforgiving darkness remained as the squeals of the creature behind him became more horrific and deafening.

Digging, digging, gouging, clawing, pulling.

The room spun and dropped. Rose and shook until Hamish no longer knew which way was up or which was down.

But still, he clawed and ripped and crawled on.

Then his hand reached out and gouged into the fleshy wood in front of him. As it did, the room froze from its spinning and trembled. Without a moment's pause, Hamish ripped out another handful. Still, unlike before, a long tendril came away with the chunk of fleshy wood. Another gouge, another lump of tendril-covered flesh, was ripped and thrown behind him. He crawled faster, not even thinking about all that was happening around or to him.

The screams from the creature behind them shifted from desperation, to anger to weak dismay.

Hamish went further and further, his determination eclipsing his pain.

Rip, gouge.

The wall he gouged in his hands went from fleshy splintered wood to fleshy meat to more of a fleshy mud. That did not stop him. Nothing would stop him.

He had no idea what he was doing or what he had done. He was fleeing for his life.

And soon, the monstrous screams behind him stopped.

Soon, the room stopped spinning.

As soon as they did... Hamish felt an insurmountable pull from far in front of him as gravity reached out.

Through the thick, gloopy mud-like wall, he felt a breeze.

THE SUN SHONE the last of its heat as dusk approached. Its rays shone a beautiful orange hue through the thick, verdant trees that grew up around this sizable grassy clearing. The temperature there was warm, very warm. It was the closest to a perfect summer's day you could get.

The sound of wildlife shimmered on the light breeze.

Birds sang.

Crickets chirped.

In the distance, a deer looked upward, alerted at something strange happening. In an instant, it bolted in the opposite direction.

Through the thick green grass, something moved.

A hand burst out of the mud, out through the grass, and grasped upward into the air in desperation.

Pulling his way out of the hole he had clawed, Hamish gasped loudly as the oxygen hit his lungs, and he tasted the fresh and clean air he had thought he would never breathe again.

He released an agonized wail as he pulled his body onto the grass.

He then saw his ankle, broken at the joint, with a small piece of thorny vine still embedded into his bone.

Panicked, he reached down and ripped the vine away from his wound without thinking of the consequences. With a primal painful yelp, he threw the remnant of the vine far away from him and scrambled backward onto the grass.

As the blood escaped from this now exposed ankle wound, Hamish's vision spun as he lost consciousness and slumped in a heap.

"HEY, KID, IT'S OKAY," said the man's voice as Hamish slowly opened his eyes. The pain in his body then collided with his consciousness and forced himself awake.

"Shhh, calm yourself." The voice said.

As Hamish tried to contain his agony, he saw a large man in his fifties, dressed in a policeman's uniform, smiling at him kindly.

"I'm gonna carry you to the hospital, okay? Don't look like you're gonna be runnin' on that any time soon."

Hamish couldn't answer as he tried to piece it all together.

"What's your name?" the man asked.

At this moment, Hamish felt his blood run cold.

"I," he managed to say with a broken and wheezing voice, "I don't know."

He did not remember. He did not remember the grotesque journey he had just made. He did not remember the dead woods, his friends, or his family. Nothing. His memories were empty.

"What's happening?" Hamish said, the tears flowing. "Where am I? Who am I? I can't remember."

Crouching down, the man put a hand on Hamish's shoulder. He looked kindly at the boy wearing the remnants of a hospital gown, covered in blood and mud, beaten, broken, helpless.

"Hey, who needs to remember?" he said calmly. "That's no fun." He then picked up Hamish, cradling him in his arms as if his five-foot-five frame weighed nothing.

Hamish exhaled painfully as he was moved.

"I know, it looks like it hurts like a son of a bitch," the man said. "But that won't last long. We'll be at the hospital in no time."

Hamish didn't reply. He was too distraught and confused.

The man began walking through the luscious thick woodland, carrying Hamish as carefully as possible.

"Let me first introduce myself. The name's Davis Eaves-Eagleton; I'm the Sheriff around here. You remember what day it is?"

Hamish shook his head, feeling each ounce of agony he had repressed before.

"Tuesday, December 29th in the year of our Lord 1924."

The next few hours were a blur.

Hamish did not recall much of the journey to the police

car, he did not recall how he got into the back seat with a blanket draped over him, but he did recollect one thing the Sheriff said before they drove off.

"This is Davis," the man said into his police radio. "I found a kid out in Cromwell Woods, taking him to the doc's now. He's banged up pretty bad."

The drive to the hospital was dark. A dreamless sleep that stole Hamish away until he was woken by the Sheriff lifting him back out of the car in front of the hospital.

The Sheriff smiled kindly. "Let's find a name for you, shall we? Can't call you nothin' after all? Everyone needs a name... even if just for a time...."

Hamish could only look back at the man, confused and afraid.

"How about Eddis? That was my Pa's name. That good for ya? We can call you E for short, as we did to him?"

Hamish did not reply as he slipped back into the darkness and dreamt of a life now forgotten.

EPILOGUE

After the horrific events in Cromwell Woods, after the cyclone of branches and creeper vines suddenly fell to the floor, after having been cut off from their life force, Findley, James, and Matt limped home battered and bruised and bleeding profusely.

After the countless investigations, protests, accusations, and despair subsided, life in the town went back to normal as possible. It took a couple of years, but soon those events were forgotten or ignored, and those that were gone were remembered and mourned silently.

People grew up. They fell in love. Got old. Passed on. The world continued to turn.

Cromwell Woods was the biggest thing to change, as over the years, somehow, the leaves grew back on its trees, grass sprouted up through the dry, dead dirt without warning, and animals soon found their way home.

Every last trace of the thing in Cromwell Woods also vanished as quickly as the survivors' wounds healed.

It was only a handful of years before the events at Hemlock Creek became legend. A ghost story amongst the young. Until the point where people doubted any of it really happened.

Even Pip Kaminsky, now confined to a wheelchair, doubted what he remembered. Despite the memories. Despite the splinters that were found in him... After the passing of the years, Pip too started to think that maybe it was indeed an animal attack.

. . .

As Sheriff Davis Eaves-Eagleton carried the nameless boy out of the woods, he had no idea what had been discarded in the grass.

As he walked away from the clearing, he did not see the piece of thorned vine that pulsed ever so slightly. The piece of sinewy wood that Hamish had torn off from his ankle.

He also did not see the blades of grass around this vine that had quickly wilted and died. He did not see that the vine had slightly grown as the life around it quickly ebbed.

Less than a month later, that whole area of grass was dead and turned to gray dirt. The life that grew there was now drained of all its energy. That small pulsing vine had also taken root from where it had fallen, and a wild thorny collection of vines grew out of it. Vines that entangled around each other into a thick dark mass. This collection of vines stood in the middle of the clearing resembling a person's silhouette.

Around the base of this plant, invisible to the human eye, a thin, yellowish mist circled.

The viny plant's root had grown downward. Deep downward. Down and down to a small mass of flesh that grew at its tip. A chunk of undulating gray, moist flesh.

**Findley, James and the Dead Woods
shall return...**

As will Emmie.

ALSO BY CHRISTIAN FRANCIS

Novels

Everyday Monsters - The Animus Chronicles Book 1

Incubus: The Descent - The Animus Chronicles Book 2

Wishmaster - The Novelization

Titan Find (AKA Creature) - The Novelization

Vamp - The Novelization

Killing Frank - The Novelization

Novellas

The Sacrifice of Anton Stacey

Graphic Novels

Hellraiser: Anthology Vol 1 & 2

Hellraiser: Bestiary Vol 4 & 6

Other

Hellbound and Damned: Three Screenplays

Printed in Great Britain
by Amazon